SWITCHING GEARS

HASBRO and its logo, TRANSFORMERS and all related characters are trademarks of Hasbro and are used with permission.
© 2011 Hasbro. All Rights Reserved.

Little, Brown and Company

Hachette Book Group
237 Park Avenue, New York, NY 10017
Visit our website at www.lb-kids.com

Little, Brown and Company is a division of Hachette Book Group, Inc. The Little, Brown name and logo are trademarks of Hachette Book Group, Inc.

The publisher is not responsible for websites (or their content) that are not owned by the publisher.

First Paperback Edition: May 2012
Originally published in hardcover in October 2011 by
Little, Brown and Company

ISBN 978-0-316-18633-9 (hc) / ISBN 978-0-316-19909-4 (pb)

10 9 8 7 6 5 4 3 2 1

RRD-C

Printed in the United States of America

SWITCHING GEARS

by Ryder Windham
with Jason Fry

LB

LITTLE, BROWN AND COMPANY
New York   Boston

CONTENTS

Chapter One
INITIAL ASSAULT

The three robots ignored the large metal signs that said RESTRICTED AREA. NO TRESPASSING. PHOTOGRAPHY PROHIBITED. The signs had been posted along the road so they could be read clearly by humans driving across the Nevada desert, but they didn't have the same impact for walking robots who stood more than thirty feet tall. Even if the robots had bothered to read the signs, they had no interest in stopping or turning back. When they left the road that evening, crushing the signs beneath their massive feet, they were determined to reach their destination.

As for photography, none of them had any interest in that, either.

"I'm just itching to test my new gun arm," said Tracer, a robot armored in sky-blue plating. Without breaking his stride, he flexed his right arm and his blunt metal fingers slid back to rearrange themselves around his wrist, revealing his built-in wide-barreled cannon.

"You call that a gun arm?" challenged Bombshock, whose highly reflective armor was dark green. "Check this out." Bombshock threw both of his bulky arms forward, and they rapidly shifted into missile launchers.

"We'll all get to use our weapons soon enough," chided the third robot, Dropshot, who was clad in gunmetal armor with white streaks and spoke in a grinding metallic voice. "After we're done with this job, you can compare firepower all night long. But right now, I'm telling both of you to keep your jaws closed and your eyes open."

Clenching his metal jaws tightly, Tracer mumbled, "'S hard to tok wid yer jawz closed."

Without moving his metal lips at all, Bombshock replied clearly, "That's okay. I can understand you."

"Shut up and walk!" Dropshot growled.

Dropshot, Bombshock, and Tracer were Decepticons, living beings from the planet Cybertron and followers of the ruthless Megatron. Their longtime enemies were another Cybertronian faction, the Autobots, who were led by Optimus Prime. Since arriving on Earth, the Decepticons had also managed to become the enemies of all human military forces.

The three Decepticons lurched forward, continuing onto the Nevada Test and Training Range, one of the largest Air Force facilities in the United States. The vast grounds contained several air bases, and the trio were heading for one in particular. They were so confident about their mission that they didn't care about the trail of large footprints they were leaving behind, or about the series of thin trip wires that stretched a few inches off the ground ahead of them. Even after their feet swept through the trip wires, they just kept walking.

Just beyond the end of a long airfield, a young airman stationed inside a wooden guard shack that had been painted white saw a light flashing on his security console. He looked closer at the monitor and saw a winking red line, which indicated that someone or something had just broken one of the many trip wires along the air base's perimeter. Noting the location of the broken trip wire, he grabbed his night-vision binoculars and stepped outside the shack to see if he could spot the trespasser. He began raising his binoculars to his eyes as he looked to the north. Seeing huge, hulking forms silhouetted against the sky about a half mile from his position, he realized he didn't need binoculars after all. He needed *help*.

Like most Air Force personnel, the airman was acutely aware that alien robots had arrived on Earth and that they could disguise themselves as ordinary cars, trucks, planes, and other vehicles. The aliens' ability to shift and change physical form down to every minute detail, creating vehicle and weapons forms, led some humans to call them Transformers, but most people who saw all the walking metal simply referred to them as giant robots.

Some robots were friendly, but others hated humans. The military worked in partnership with a few, but they had also engaged in recent deadly battles with others. Because the airman had not been notified about any robots visiting the airfield, he had to assume these three were hostile.

Keeping his eyes on the approaching forms, the airman tapped his headset and said, "Cactus station nine to base. I've got a visual on three giant robots approaching from the north. I repeat, three giant robots approaching from the north."

A siren began blaring behind the airman. Then he heard a familiar noise of engines. He glanced back and saw the headlights of armored personnel carriers moving past the blinking lights of the airfield, and then a trio of F-22 fighter planes buzzed above him, heading north. Keeping his eyes fixed on the fighters, he turned his head to watch them race toward the approaching robots.

The first F-22 opened fire, launching a missile that streaked toward the lead intruder. The robot shifted his massive upper body with surprising speed to dodge the missile, which sped past him and grazed the leg of one of his companions before it traveled an additional five hundred feet and smashed into the ground. The F-22s had already peeled away from the robots when the missile detonated. The power of the blast was close enough that the airman felt the shock wave, which sent him stumbling backward into the door of his guard post.

When the airman recovered, he looked back and saw that the robot who'd been struck was down on one knee. The robot was close enough that the airman could see he was green. The airman watched the other two robots turn their huge heads to look back at their fallen comrade while they continued walking. The green robot rose, tested his leg, and then moved after the others to rejoin them as they continued their steady march toward the airfield.

"Cactus station nine to base!" the airman shouted into his headset. "Strike unsuccessful! Repeat, strike unsuccessful! They're still coming!" Knowing that the metal giants would not have any difficulty reducing the guard shack to splinters, the airman ran for cover.

Dropshot paused to scan the night sky, then raised one long metal arm. His fist blossomed into a fireball of energy that launched into the darkness. The brilliant projectile streaked toward the jet fighter that had struck Bombshock. Dropshot leered with pleasure as the projectile struck its mark and blew it out of the sky.

The two remaining jets veered away from the explosion. Bombshock adjusted his targeting sensors as he raised his arms and crossed them in front of his armored chest, then fired two heat-seeking missiles to the left and right. The missiles zipped through the night sky, racing after the fleeing jet fighters. A moment later, two explosions rained shattered pieces down upon the desert.

"I hate organic life-forms," Dropshot muttered.

"Nice shooting, Bombshock," Tracer said.

Bombshock chuckled. "Swatting insects is fun!" Seeing human soldiers approaching from the air base, he said, "Oh, good! Here come more!"

"Let's move," Dropshot said. "Remember, those organics aren't the only ones watching us." The machines lowered their arms and continued to the base.

Far away from the battle in the desert, on a small rise that overlooked the distant airfield, a man named Simon Clay lowered his high-powered binoculars. He was smiling because he'd just seen the robots shoot down the three F-22s.

Clay stood a short distance from his van, which was parked behind a wide rock formation. The van had a matte black paint job that made it hard to be seen at night and also difficult to find on satellite photos. It had a tough suspension and armored tires that would allow him to race across rough terrain if he needed to clear out in a hurry. The van was filled with communications gear, and a small but powerful satellite dish stuck up through a hatch in the roof. Clay's equipment was as good as anything the U.S. government possessed. He knew the Air Force officials would have been very interested to know why that gear was trained on the battle unfolding on the out-skirts of the Nevada Test and Training Range. He was equally sure the Air Force would never know about him or his van.

Clay's walkie-talkie buzzed. He knew the transmission was from Dropshot. He was still smiling as he held the walkie-talkie up to his mouth and said, "This is Stealth One. Go ahead."

Dropshot replied, "The organics are scram-bling ground units to engage us." The walkie-talkie's encryption software made Dropshot's metallic voice sound even harsher than it did in person.

11

"Roger that, Dropshot," Clay said. "Stay on objective. Eliminate anything that gets in your way."

"The organics are delaying their ground deployment," Dropshot said. "They may be preparing carbon-fiber encasement canisters."

Clay thought he heard concern in Dropshot's voice, and his smile vanished. He understood that refrigerated carbon fiber could trap a robot's metal limbs in a rapidly hardening shell, immobilizing them, and that it was one of the more successful defenses against hostile Cybertronians. He also knew the robots didn't have all night to do what needed to be done. "Your emergency heat couplers were tested this morning, Dropshot," he said impatiently. "Quit stalling and complete the mission. Stealth One out."

"Acknowledged," the Decepticon grumbled.

Clay returned his walkie-talkie to his belt

clip and raised the binoculars to his eyes again. He didn't trust the Decepticons. They frightened him. Considering that they were giant armored robots with destructive weapons built into their bodies, he believed his fear was justified. However, for the moment, he was the one giving them the orders.

Peering through the binoculars, he watched the robots in the distance as they moved closer to the airfield, where a few dozen military vehicles were driving toward a guard shack. When he saw Dropshot shatter the shack with a single kick, his mouth twitched back into a cruel smile.

The airman who'd abandoned the now-ruined shack jumped onto one of the armored personnel carriers moving across the airfield. In the APC turrets, grim-faced gunners targeted the invaders who had already brought down three jet fighters.

Five hundred feet away from the APCs, Dropshot's lenses whirred as his ocular sensors scanned each vehicle. His infrared sensor showed no cool spots that could be refrigerated carbon-fiber tanks, only the crimson blobs of frightened, sweating organics. In a nanosecond, Dropshot's onboard data processors assigned threat levels to each target and relayed the information to Bombshock and Tracer.

Bombshock and Tracer grinned. According to Dropshot, none of the pathetic species of insects called humans could hurt the Decepticons, including the ones in the armored vehicles.

"Fire when ready," Dropshot growled. He raised one arm, bracketed the lead APC in his sights, and unlocked his trigger actuators. He opened fire, and the soldiers fired back.

On a service road that ran along the outer perimeter of the Nevada Test and Training Range, a white SUV came to a sudden stop. The driver had been startled by the bright bursts of light in the black sky over the desert. His family was already upset with him because they were pretty sure he had taken a very wrong turn for Las Vegas, but he couldn't be faulted for failing to see the Air Force's warning signs that had been recently crushed by enormous trespassers.

His wife followed his gaze to the distant bursts of light. The driver yelled, "Cody! Stop watching that DVD for a minute!"

"Aw, Dad," complained the boy, who sat in the backseat. "Not more *nature*."

"This is better than nature! It's fireworks!"

"Where?" The boy turned his attention away from the DVD player secured to the back of his father's seat just in time to see a series of bright explosions ripple across the sky. The explosions illuminated three giant robots striding across the desert.

"Whoa," said the driver's wife. "I don't think those are fireworks."

Taking a sudden interest in the world outside the SUV's air-conditioned interior, the boy in the backseat set his cell phone on video mode, rolled down his window, and began recording the distant robots. "I can't wait to post this on my blog!"

"The heck you're posting it on your blog!" the boy's mother said as she reached for her own cell phone. "TV networks will *pay* for this video!"

And then the family saw something else in the sky: the lights of an approaching aircraft.

The Decepticon called Tracer was firing at the Air Force's fleeing armored vehicles when he spotted the incoming plane. He transmitted a data burst to Dropshot, who turned to face west, his ocular sensors whirring as they focused on the rapidly approaching airborne target. It was a large military transport aircraft. The aircraft was almost directly overhead when its aft section opened and two large vehicles tumbled out. The first vehicle was a dark blue semitruck with red flames painted on the cab. The second vehicle was a black medium-duty pickup truck.

Dropshot recognized both vehicles immediately and knew they were more than just trucks. He switched over to his external comm channel, the one he shared with the arrogant human named Simon Clay. Dropshot made no attempt to conceal his anger as he growled, "You told us we would *not* encounter Autobots!"

Chapter Two
RESCUE OP

The dark blue semitruck that fell from the military aircraft was actually the Autobot leader, Optimus Prime, another sentient being from Cybertron. His companion, the black pickup truck, was Optimus's friend and Cybertronian compatriot, an Autobot named Ironhide, a weapons specialist who enjoyed exercising his trigger fingers. Their aircraft had been supplied by NEST.

Only military personnel knew that NEST was

an acronym for Non-biological Extraterrestrial Species Treaty. The Autobots were working with the U.S. armed forces to defend Earth against Decepticons such as the three giant robots currently attacking the Nevada air base directly below Optimus Prime and Ironhide.

Still falling from the aircraft, the two disguised Autobots began changing, shifting and flipping metal panels as they rearranged their physical configurations to reveal themselves as large robot-looking figures. Although each Autobot body had a head atop a torso with two arms and two legs, the Autobots were amused that people referred to their anatomy as humanoid because the Cybertronian species predated human existence.

Optimus Prime and Ironhide activated the parachutes they'd secured onto their backs. The chutes deployed with loud pops as they caught the air, and the two Autobots maneuvered to land on the ground between the three Decepticons and the human soldiers. Descending alongside his larger friend, Ironhide flexed his two arm-mounted cannons and said, "This is gonna be fun."

"Watch out for the soldiers," Optimus Prime said. He had known Ironhide for many years, and they had fought side by side in battles on dozens of worlds. Although he trusted the scarred old Autobot with his life, Optimus was still quick to reproach Ironhide for getting overly enthusiastic in a brawl.

Optimus radioed a quick transmission to the authorities at the Nevada Test and Training Range, warning them to pull back their APCs and not to fire on him or Ironhide. He then directed his sensors to sort through the babble of transmissions that were being broadcast across the area. In mere seconds, his cognitive modules sifted through millions of telephone calls, radio feeds, e-mail conversations, and text messages. He discarded the usual human chatter that made up more than 99.99 percent of the transmissions and focused on what was left.

His human allies at NEST had supplied him with the U.S. military codes encrypting their communications, saving him several seconds of computing time. That left two communications channels to investigate. The first one featured three sources of nanoburst communications generated by the Decepticons and guarded by quantum encryption ciphers that his processors estimated would take an Earth computer 1.4 million years to crack. The other channel was encrypted using human technology. Optimus broke all the codes in less than two seconds. He reviewed the last ten minutes of communications he had recorded in that vulnerable channel, prioritized the interesting material, and transmitted details to Ironhide.

"Thanks for the info, boss," Ironhide replied as he adjusted his descent. "How do you want to play this game?"

"The Decepticon called Bombshock has suffered slight to moderate damage to the right knee. Leave him for last. I will take Dropshot. Tracer is yours."

"Aw, boss," Ironhide groaned. "I could take all three of them while you buffed out some dings."

"Overconfidence is not the soldier's way," Optimus said. "And remember, do not harm the humans."

Ironhide chuckled. "*Their* job is to stay out of my way!"

Decepticon missiles whizzed past the Autobots as they neared the ground. Both Autobots cut their chutes and hit the airfield running. Optimus went straight for Dropshot while Ironhide ran toward Tracer. Bombshock was two hundred feet away from his allies, but the Autobots saw him limping toward Dropshot.

The lead Decepticon had just enough time to assume a defensive stance before Optimus's giant metal foot caught him in the chest plate, driving him into the ground and sending a wave of dirt and tumbleweeds skyward. Dropshot rolled as Optimus hit him and managed to launch a kick that hit Optimus's back. Losing his balance, Optimus stumbled and somersaulted across the airfield.

"Rough landing, boss!" Ironhide said as he ducked a swarm of missiles that Tracer had fired. Ironhide rushed the sky-blue Decepticon and tackled him. The motors in their arms strained as they wrestled. Tracer's forearm cannon spat fire, blasting craters into the ground around them.

Optimus rolled up from the ground just in time to see Dropshot coming at him fast. The Autobot leader extended the barrage cannon housed in his right shoulder and fired at Dropshot, who flung himself sideways. The blast sailed past Dropshot, but as he swung his body around to resume his attack, Optimus's fist caved into the armor protecting the Decepticon's left shoulder.

Dropshot howled in pain. Optimus grabbed his opponent's right forearm with both of his metal hands. Motors screamed as Dropshot tried to bring his left arm up but found it blocked by his now-buckled shoulder armor. Without losing his grip on Dropshot, Optimus shouted, "Ironhide! Bombshock is closing ground!"

Ironhide chuckled. "Let me know when you're done playin' with your friend and we'll take

Bombshock out together." With a roar of servos, Ironhide brought a knee up into Tracer's midsection. Tracer squealed as his feet left the ground. Ironhide seized Tracer's torso, lifted him overhead, and then turned and hurled him into the limping Bombshock. The two Decepticons crashed to the ground.

Dropshot tried to wriggle out of Optimus's grip, but the Autobot wrenched his opponent's left arm up behind his back. Optimus said, "It doesn't have to be like this, Dropshot. You don't *have* to believe the lies of Megatron."

Dropshot let out a mechanized snort, then wrenched his right arm free and aimed his cannons at a cluster of soldiers standing on the far side of the airfield. As Dropshot charged his cannons, Optimus did not have to make any calculations to know that soldiers would die if Dropshot fired. The mighty Autobot recalibrated his own right arm into the form of a large blade, which he then drove down through Dropshot's chest.

"No!" Tracer screamed as he saw sparks explode from Dropshot's body. Dropshot's right wrist spun wildly before the light in his eyes winked out and his limbs went limp. Tracer jumped to his feet, leaving Bombshock as he tried to run past Ironhide to get a clear shot at Optimus. Bombshock's damaged knee whined in protest as he tried to get up.

Before Tracer could bring his weapons to bear, Ironhide pivoted at the waist and head-butted the Decepticon, knocking him down again. Tracer tumbled and rolled, but when he came to a stop in a crouched position, he was staring up into the barrel of the large fission chamber on Ironhide's left arm.

Large metal chunks of Tracer's shattered

armor whipped through the air, and a few bits went soaring over a stranded APC. Seeing a frightened soldier huddled beside the APC, Ironhide commented, "First rule of the battlefield: Know when to duck!"

Leaving the remains of Dropshot, Optimus walked across the airfield to join Ironhide. Bombshock looked from one Autobot to the other as he tried to decide his next course of action. Hearing Optimus approach, Ironhide said, "You're not going to try negotiating with this hopeless loser, are you, boss?"

"There is always hope," Optimus said as he retracted his blade and extended an open hand to the remaining Decepticon. "Bombshock, you can stop —"

Bombshock fired one of his missile launchers. Three projectiles went wild into the night, arcing over the air base. The missiles were still soaring when Bombshock, with a desperate gleam in his red eyes, swung both arms out so his missile launchers were aimed at structures on the far side of the airfield. The three already-fired missiles descended and smashed into the desert floor, causing a large explosion that kicked up sand in all directions. Jutting his narrow metal chin at the airfield's structures, Bombshock faced Optimus and said, "Take one more step, and I'll destroy those buildings and everyone in them!"

"Remember how we did it at the Battle of Polyhex?" Ironhide asked his leader.

Polyhex had been a province on Cybertron, and the site of several battles. Keeping his blue eyes fixed on Bombshock, Optimus answered, "*Which* Battle of Polyhex?"

"The second one," Ironhide said as he cycled through his weapons systems.

Optimus nodded. "I remember." Optimus

assumed an offensive stance, catching Bomb-shock's attention, at the same moment that Ironhide dived to the Decepticon's right side. In an effort to keep both Autobots in view, Bomb-shock turned to his right, too, but his damaged knee locked with a screech. Before Bombshock could fire, Optimus deployed his battle blade again and charged.

The blade plunged through Bombshock's chest as Optimus threw his own bulk against the Decepticon. Bombshock's arms jerked away from his body, and he reflexively fired three more missiles as he fell lifeless to the ground. Like the previous three missiles, they missed their mark. They sputtered flames as they raced away from the airfield, then angled up into the air before they detonated in quick succession.

"Except for the *boom-boom-boom* part," Ironhide said, watching the fiery remnants of the explosion, "that was *exactly* how we did it at Polyhex." Feeling pleased and proud, he raised one fist and thumped his metal chest with a loud clang, then turned and waved to the soldiers who were climbing out of their armored personnel carriers. The soldiers responded with riotous cheers. Ironhide's metal mouth twisted into a grin. "Maybe the Air Force will give us medals for winning this fight."

Optimus looked at Bombshock's motionless body and shook his head sadly. "It's too early to celebrate, Ironhide." Lifting his gaze, Optimus surveyed the dark landscape beyond the airfield. "When we landed, I intercepted a transmission."

But Ironhide was already walking with great lumbering strides to meet the crowd of soldiers who had emerged from their APCs. Some of the soldiers looked frightened, but many were excited by the astonishing victory they'd just witnessed.

"We don't get enough photo ops," Ironhide said as he flexed his metal arms. "Wait till they get a load of these cannons!"

"The battle was unimportant," Optimus said as he came up behind him. "What matters is the transmission I intercepted. These Decepticons were not working alone. They were in communication with a secret ally."

"Well, their secret ally can report they got spanked," Ironhide crowed. "When I tell Bumblebee and Ratchet about this brawl, they're gonna be sorry they missed it!"

On a distant ridge, Simon Clay lowered his binoculars. He was no longer smiling. He returned to his van, shut the roof hatch, clambered into the driver's seat, and sped away in a shower of dirt and gravel. Gripping the steering wheel with one hand, he clutched his cell phone with the other and thumbed a single button.

"Go ahead," said a voice on the other end of the line.

Clay recognized the voice as Stealth Leader, whom he'd never met face-to-face. The voice was so disguised by electronic modulation that Clay couldn't tell whether Stealth Leader was male, female, or even human. Trying to force himself to stay calm, Clay said, "Things didn't go as expected."

No response.

"All three assets were lost," Clay said.

"Get off the phone. And stay off it. Return to base immediately."

Clay heard the connection break. He swallowed hard and kept driving.

Chapter Three
HOUSE PARTY

As soon as twelve-year-old Kevin Bowman heard the heavy metal music blasting out of the loudspeakers, he knew that coming over to Gilbert Poole's house had been a big, big mistake.

In all fairness, Gilbert—Kevin's friend and classmate at Hurley's Crossing Middle School—hadn't known there was going to be a party at his house, either. The metal band in the backyard and the teenagers singing loudly and very off-key in the swimming pool were a surprise to him, too, as was the limo, catering crew, and "mocktail" bartender, all of which had arrived at the house within the past twenty minutes. Still, it did not change the fact that Kevin had not ridden his bike all the way to Gilbert's house to have fun. He'd come to Gilbert's house because they were supposed to be working on a science project together.

And their assignment was due on Monday.

"I can't hear myself think," Kevin said.

"What?" Gilbert shouted.

"Forget it," Kevin muttered. They went up to Gilbert's cluttered bedroom, where piled-up homework fought for space on a desk filled with action figures and baseball cards. Kevin looked out the window at the crazy scene in the backyard. The limo belonged to Douglas

Porter, who was seventeen years old and beyond stinking rich. Gilbert's older sister, Charlene, was Douglas Porter's girlfriend.

"What's the occasion?" Kevin shouted.

Gilbert answered, "What?"

"*Why is this party going on?*" Kevin screamed.

"My sister's birthday."

Turning away from the window, Kevin said, "You told me Charlene's birthday was next week."

Gilbert shrugged. "I guess when you're Douglas Porter, people's birthdays are whenever you say they are." Gilbert flopped down on his bed and ran a hand through his mop of brown hair.

Kevin looked out the window again and said, "I'll bet your parents will flip out when they get home."

"They're gone for the weekend. Went off to Vegas."

Lifting his eyebrows in surprise, Kevin asked, "Do they know about this party?"

Gilbert nodded. "Douglas asked permission to throw a little party for Charlene, and then he gave my parents an all-expenses-paid trip to Vegas. Key word: *little*. He didn't say anything about caterers or a band."

"Enough about Douglas Porter and his money," Kevin said. "We have work to do." He perched on the desk chair as he opened his backpack and got out the work he'd done so far on their science project. Gilbert's idea was to show how stars that appeared to be close together in Earth's night sky were actually millions of light-years apart in space. Kevin wanted to create a series of diagrams to show how the movement of the stars warped and bent constellations over time, and would eventually stretch the Big Dipper like taffy until it didn't look like a dipper at all.

Unfortunately, both of them had overlooked an important part of the assignment until today. The science project was supposed to have a practical application for everyday life.

"How about this?" Gilbert said. "What if we show how the constellations help psychics and astronomers predict the future and stuff?"

"*Astrologers,* not astronomers," Kevin said. "And you can forget about that. This assignment has to be *practical.* If psychics and astrologers could really predict the future, then everyone would know about bad things before they happened. Like your sister's party, for example."

"Gimme a break!" Gilbert moaned. "I told you, I didn't know about the party."

Disgusted, Kevin threw his pencil down on

Gilbert's desk. It wiggled across the desk in time with the vibrations from the music in the backyard. He glanced out the window and saw headlights. More limos were pulling up to the house. "This must have cost a lot, even for Douglas," he said.

Gilbert nodded. "That's Douglas for ya. Money doesn't matter. I heard his father's company is worth billions."

"What's the name of the company again?"

"Hyperdynamix. I think they do some kind of military work. I asked Douglas about it once, but he said he didn't care what his father did, just so long as it kept him up to his neck in money."

The band finished their ravaging of a classic song by the Beach Boys, and the audience responded with applause and enthusiastic hoots. A moment later, the band's lead singer yelled,

"How about a big hand for our host, Douglas Porter!"

Kevin scowled. "Whatever Hyperdynamix does, it's definitely profitable."

"What?" Gilbert said.

Kevin rolled his eyes. Raising his voice, he said, "If we're not going to get any work done, we might as well get a soda and some food."

"I was thinking the same thing," Gilbert said as he led Kevin out of his room. "Heck, Douglas paid for everything. And I wouldn't want to let any food go to waste!"

The living room was filled with older teens. Some were locals whom Kevin recognized from Hurley's Crossing; others were out-of-towners he'd never seen before. The out-of-towners wore designer T-shirts and expensive sneakers. The band started playing again as Kevin and Gilbert approached the bartender whom Douglas had hired, and the noise forced Kevin and Gilbert to yell out their orders.

Kevin got his Coke and turned around to see that several partyers had piled onto the couch in front of an enormous television. He didn't recognize any of them. They were lazily flipping channels as they shouted at one another. A group of girls came running through the living room, trailing water from the pool. They were all wearing bikinis.

"Oh, man," Gilbert said. "Look at that."

"Look at what?"

"On TV."

Kevin looked at the TV screen. The news was on. He saw a map of Nevada with an X in the southern part of the state, east of Hurley's Crossing. Although the noise from the party made it impossible to hear the newscaster's voice, Kevin could clearly read the caption at

the bottom of the screen. The big, bold letters
were trumpeting a breaking-news story:

Amateur Video — Giant Robots Attack Air Force Training Area

Eyes glued to the TV screen, Kevin froze. He
hated giant robots.

Chapter Four
INCOMING!

At Edwards Air Force Base in California, inside the ordinary-looking hangar that was actually NEST Forward Strike Base, Autobots Bumblebee and Ratchet faced a television monitor to watch the news report of giant robots sighted at the Nevada Test and Training Range. Earlier, they had received a classified report about what had really transpired—that their allies Optimus Prime and Ironhide had foiled a surprise Decepticon attack.

Bumblebee was a bright yellow Autobot scout whose height was sixteen feet and two inches. Like his Autobot friends, he was a veteran of the climactic battle at Tyger Pax on Cybertron. During that battle, the Decepticon leader, Megatron, had crushed Bumblebee's vocal processor, rendering him mute. After arriving on Earth, Bumblebee used his trans-scanning technology to allow himself to shift into a sporty two-door car with stripes, and he became quite adept at communicating with humans by way of playing selected lyrics from popular songs on his radio. His built-in weaponry included a magnetic field generator and a mortar delivery system.

Ratchet, who stood just over twenty feet tall, could change into a distinctive military rescue vehicle that was detailed with bright red stripes. As he watched the television with Bumblebee, he repeatedly extended and retracted his buzz-saw attachment, verifying that the mechanism's pistons and guides were working properly. Finding all the components working to his satisfaction, Ratchet activated the saw, and its whine rose to a shriek as he brought it up to full power.

Glancing at the shrieking saw, Bumblebee transmitted a short-range communications burst that only Ratchet could understand. *"You're scaring our friends."*

Receiving this, Ratchet looked around the hangar and realized the NEST techs were glancing at him nervously. Although the saw attachment was meant for battlefield repairs, Ratchet realized that humans might be intimidated by the sight of an immense robot with a massive spinning saw at the end of one arm, especially if the techs knew that the saw had been used as a weapon against a large number of Decepticons.

Embarrassed, Ratchet shut down the saw and retracted it back into his arm. "Just to remind you," he said to the human techs, "I'm a medical officer by training and a soldier by circumstances."

After the television news report about the sightings in Nevada was over, Bumblebee gurgled in a distorted voice that was as slow as it was deep. "I'mmmm—sorrrrrrrrrrr..." Bumblebee stopped and hung his head in frustration. Recent attempts to fix his vocal processor hadn't succeeded any more than previous efforts. Switching back to electronic signals, he faced Ratchet and transmitted, *"I'm sorry we missed that fight in the desert. Looked like Ironhide got under the boss's skin!"*

"Sometimes, I think that's Ironhide's primary function," Ratchet replied drily.

A NEST technician hurried over to Ratchet

and gazed at him curiously. The man was wearing the insignia of the team's satellite-tracking division. Ratchet gazed down at the technician. "Yes?"

"We picked up two meteoroids on the monitors. They're both on a trajectory for Earth, about ten minutes apart. Based on their current course, we anticipate touchdown somewhere in central Nevada."

Ratchet and Bumblebee looked at each other, then glanced back at the television screen that they'd just been watching. Returning his attention to the technician, Ratchet said, "The Decepticon attack was in Nevada. Do you think the incoming meteoroids are transition forms?"

"That is our assumption," said the technician, who was aware of how Cybertronians crossed space in elongated metallic forms that resembled comets or meteors before they landed on planets. After landing, the Cybertronians then reconfigured their bodies into their protoforms and used their trans-scanning technology to reformat themselves into vehicles that suited their personalities.

Bumblebee faced the technician and burbled, "Auttttttttooooo...?"

"We don't know if they're Autobots or Decepticons," the technician said. "Major Lennox wants a contact team airborne and on standby to investigate the crash sites. With Optimus Prime and Ironhide stuck in debriefing, he requests that you two join them in—"

Before the technician could finish, Bumblebee fired up his speakers, played a snippet of a bouncy tune, and began skipping along to the beat. Ratchet held up a hand for silence, not to discourage Bumblebee's enthusiasm but because he hated that particular tune. "I *know* you're excited, Bumblebee," Ratchet said. With a metal thumb aimed back at the television monitor, he added, "Maybe you'll get a chance to fight in Nevada after all!"

Chapter Five
FIRE IN THE SKY

Giant robots.

Kevin Bowman was oblivious to the loud music and everyone else in Gilbert Poole's house. His eyes remained fixed on the television. The video images were shaky, but they showed enough. Distant figures moved in the dark, lit up by the occasional fire bursts. Someone must have hit the mute button because the television's closed captioning was on, allowing Kevin to follow the news reporter's narration even though he couldn't hear it.

YOU ARE LOOKING AT VIDEO FOOTAGE JUST TAKEN BY A TOURIST FAMILY DRIVING ON A HIGHWAY EAST OF THE BATTLE ZONE. SEEING WHAT THEY THOUGHT WAS FIREWORKS, THE FAMILY PULLED OVER ON THE SIDE OF THE ROAD. BUT THESE ARE MORE THAN FIREWORKS. IN THIS NEXT SHOT, AN EXPLOSION IN THE BACKGROUND CLEARLY SHOWS THREE GIANT ROBOTIC BEINGS SIMILAR TO THE ONES PREVIOUSLY SEEN—

The channel changed to a reality show. A bald man was eating a bucketful of large bugs.

"Hey!" Kevin yelled, loud enough to be heard over the band. "Put it back!" He scanned the living room, trying to figure out who was holding the remote control for the television. And then he spotted him.

Douglas Porter, the billionaire's son. He was

among the people seated on the couch in front of the television, easily distinguishable by his perfect hair and gleaming white teeth. Douglas held up the remote so Kevin could see it, then looked at Kevin and laughed.

"Knock it off!" Kevin said. "Go back to the news!"

Next to Kevin, Gilbert cleared his throat. "Whoa, Kevin, what's going on?"

Douglas turned off the television, tossed the remote onto the coffee table, and pronounced, "I'm bored." He looked back, noticed Kevin glaring at him, and said, "What's with you?"

Charlene came into the room with a towel wrapped around her body. She noticed the tension immediately and blamed her little brother. "Gilbert! What's your friend doing?"

Kevin was suddenly aware that the band had stopped playing and that other kids in the living room were now looking at him. He said, "I was just…watching the news. Giant robots were attacking—"

"News?" Douglas laughed again. "That was just some movie. Either that or a really long trailer for a movie. Giant robots? Spare me!"

Kevin raised his eyebrows. "Oh? Then what happened at Mission City? In Egypt? And who sent that transmission to every TV around the world? Was *that* a movie, too?" Kevin had no doubt that everyone in the room would know what he was talking about. The video of an evil robot making demands was easily available on YouTube, and it had caused widespread panic before news reports made it clear that he had been defeated in a fierce desert battle. Closer to home, the skirmish in Mission City also had rough videos online. Not that Kevin could bear to watch them.

"Are you serious?" Douglas laughed again. "Don't tell me you believe that conspiracy-theory stuff about Earth being invaded by alien robots." He shook his head without disturbing his perfect hair. "You're crazy."

Two girls sitting on the couch giggled. Charlene glared at them, then glared back at Kevin and Gilbert. Her eyes said, *Stop ruining my party right now.* Gilbert tugged at his elbow, but Kevin shook him off and leaned forward. "Even the government has admitted—"

"Come on, Kevin," Gilbert interrupted. "Let's just get out of—"

"What happened in Mission City," Douglas continued, "had nothing to do with aliens. But hey, if you want to go around thinking that the crazy stuff that conspiracy nuts write on the Internet is true, you go right ahead. It's a free country."

"Oh, yeah?" Kevin said. "If you know what *really* happened in Mission City, why don't you tell us? I'd love to hear it." He couldn't believe this guy. Most people accepted that these alien beings existed. Sure, a few insisted the whole alien robot thing was a hoax, like the moon landing, but they were usually weirdos. How could Douglas, the sophisticated rich kid, think this was made up?

"Gladly," Douglas said. Rising from the couch, he looked at the other teens in the room and grinned, happy to have their attention. He appeared to notice Charlene for the first time and went over to drape his arm around her shoulder. "The robots that made the news in Mission City were just a bunch of experimental rescue robots created by defense contractors right here in Nevada. The only reason they made the news was because they malfunctioned. And the damage that they caused? That was way, way exaggerated."

Gilbert gasped. Charlene had the grace to shrug off Douglas and shake her head as she looked at the floor. They both knew what the Mission City disaster meant to Kevin.

Kevin felt his face flush, and he blinked to keep the tears from welling up in his eyes. Struggling to keep his voice from quavering, he said, "*Exaggerated*, huh? Then tell me something else, Douglas. My parents were in Mission City. Were their *deaths* exaggerated, too?"

Everyone in the room looked from Kevin to Douglas. The sneering grin had vanished. He dragged his fingers through his perfect hair and said quietly, "I'm sorry. I didn't know."

"That's right," Kevin said. "You don't know. But I do. I *know* these giant robots exist. I *know* because they *killed my parents*." He turned and pushed past some gawkers who'd been standing behind him as he headed for the door. Gilbert followed.

"Come on, Kev, he said he was sorry. Why don't we just—"

"Forget it, Gilbert," Kevin said as he opened the front door. "I'm going home."

Riding his bike, Kevin traveled along the dusty stretch of land to the east of Hurley's Crossing, keeping off the road because it was after dark. He was still really angry that Douglas Porter had tried to dismiss the Mission City disaster as "exaggerated."

What a jerk.

Kevin had a cell phone in his pocket, and he thought about calling his older brother, Duane.

He wanted to know if Duane had seen the news report about the robots at the Air Force base, but Duane was probably busy at his job at the Hawthorne Army Depot, north of Hurley's Crossing. When he thought about how Duane was doing his second week of night shifts, Kevin decided to leave him alone.

A lot of people in Hurley's Crossing worked at Hawthorne. Kevin and Duane's parents had worked there for years, until the attack in Mission City changed everything. Duane had become Kevin's guardian and was currently juggling jobs at Hawthorne and the local minimart while keeping careful track of the life insurance money their parents had left behind. Kevin tried to help by doing his homework and his share of the chores without needing to be asked and relying on his much-repaired bike for transportation. He'd learned to take care of himself so his brother would have a little less to worry about.

Kevin decided he would talk with Duane about the news report in the morning. Meanwhile, he had to figure out some way to salvage the science project that he should have completed already. Thinking about giant robots when he should be thinking about the stars wasn't going to help.

Kevin stopped his bike and looked up. There wasn't a single cloud in the night sky, which was filled with stars. A crescent moon was suspended to the west. Years ago, on cool evenings in his backyard, Kevin's mother had taught him and Duane what she knew about astronomy, which had been plenty. Kevin looked up to spot the stars he knew by name. Aldebaran in the constellation Taurus, and Betelgeuse and Rigel in Orion. To Kevin, seeing those stars and constellations was like seeing old friends.

His mom had told him that Betelgeuse was an old star, in the last stages of life. It might even have already used up its fuel and become a supernova. If that titanic explosion had happened, no human being knew it yet. Betelgeuse was so far away that its light took hundreds of years to reach Earth. Kevin had daydreamed about what it would be like to look up and see a supernova, a new light in the sky, bright as a full moon. Those lucky enough to see it would remember it forever.

He recalled asking his science teacher last year about the possibility of seeing a supernova. She'd listened with a bored look on her face, then pointed out that it was unlikely it would happen anytime soon, or even in their lifetimes, so there was no point in talking about it. Kevin had countered that *unlikely* wasn't the same as *impossible*. For his trouble, he got an extra homework assignment.

His eyes flicked to the Big Dipper, an asterism, or a pattern of stars, that was part of the Great Bear constellation. Mariners and explorers had used their own asterisms and the constellations to navigate for centuries. Kevin had considered making his science project about using stars for navigation, but it was Gilbert who'd pointed out that Global Positioning Systems had gotten rid of the need to use the stars for directions. If people wanted directions, they just consulted the GPS in their cars or in their smartphones.

We're going to get a C, worried Kevin. And then he saw a ball of light streaking across the sky. He knew at once that it was a meteor, and he watched in amazement as it appeared to grow larger and brighter. He heard an increasingly loud *whoosh* and realized he was actually hearing the meteor burn through the atmosphere. The glowing ball hurtled past the ridge to the east, near the river, and vanished in the dark landscape. A moment later, Kevin heard the impact, dulled by distance but still sounding like a muffled *boom*.

Straddling his bike, Kevin thought for a moment about going home or calling Gilbert but immediately decided against both. He shifted his bike's front tire and started pedaling madly in the direction of the ridge. Something that big wouldn't have just vaporized on impact. There would be a meteorite left behind, or maybe pieces of it. Kevin's mother had told him that meteorites could be very valuable.

Racing into the night, he felt more excited

than he had in years. He hoped he would be the first to find the meteorite. If it was worth a lot of money, then his brother would be able to quit one of his jobs.

And if he did discover a meteorite, Kevin was pretty sure it would get him an A on his science project.

Chapter Six
CONTACT

High above western Nevada, a jet-black military helicopter zoomed through the night. In the cargo hold, illuminated by red emergency lighting, a squad of soldiers checked their weapons while casting occasional glances at the large forms of Bumblebee and Ratchet. The two Autobots' magnetic feet kept them firmly affixed to the deck, and they appeared to be relaxed, standing still with their arms folded, like veteran sailors on a boat in rough seas.

A NEST technician yelled up at Bumblebee and Ratchet, "We've plotted the impact site of the first meteoroid. It's east of a town called Hurley's Crossing. Our estimated time of arrival is twenty minutes. Base command will advise on the location of the second impact site once it's known."

The technician had not told the two Autobots anything they didn't already know. Both Bumblebee and Ratchet had been using their transmitters to tap into the same stream of NEST data that the technician had accessed, but they nodded politely and Ratchet said, "Twenty minutes, huh? Thanks for telling us."

Bumblebee sifted through several dozen radio frequencies before he found what he thought was an appropriate song for the occasion. He tilted his head back and broadcast a man's raspy voice crooning, "*We have all the time in the world.*"

"Let's hope so," Ratchet replied. "A lot of things can happen in twenty minutes."

Kevin Bowman had no difficulty finding the impact site. All he'd had to do was ride his bike toward the river, then follow the deep furrow the meteorite had carved in the ground. Stopping his bike on a road atop a ridge where only parched grass grew, he saw that the meteorite's trail ended near an old abandoned shed and a farmhouse, which had been built decades ago, when the river had run higher. A tree that rose up from within the farmhouse's walls was evidence that the structure's roof was a thing of the past, too.

Kevin dipped his hand into a pocket and removed his cell phone, then began fiddling with the phone's camera settings. He didn't know if he could get a decent picture of the impact site before walking down for a closer look, but he wanted to try. He had an old phone, and the camera wasn't that great, so he rarely used it. He was still trying to puzzle out the controls when he heard a strange whine. Lifting his gaze from his phone, he saw a massive shape rise out of the crater.

Kevin gasped. *A robot!*

It was taller than the farmhouse, and its metal body was a mass of pistons and gears and blinking lights. Atop the wide silver chest sat a relatively small head. As the robot flexed its shiny, reddish limbs and shrugged its massive shoulders, it resembled a person getting up from a nap.

Hoping to avoid being seen, Kevin threw himself sideways, bringing his bike with him. He landed on his left side, taking care not to lose his grip on his phone or let the bike bounce off the road and make any noise. He watched the hulking form step out of the crater.

The robot's gears whined as it inspected the roofless house. It reached out to the tree that had grown within the house, and brushed the backs of its metal fingers against the tree's leaves. Then the robot turned to examine the half-tumbled-down shed, which housed a rusted tractor. Beside the shed, an old sport utility vehicle had been stripped of its tires and rested on cinder blocks. The robot pinged the roof of the SUV with its finger.

Kevin lay sprawled on the ground, every muscle tense as he tried to stay still and hold his bike. He heard a low hum, which he suspected came from the robot. Remembering his cell phone, he decided he could call 911 and tell the police that there was another giant on the loose, just like the robots he'd seen on the news earlier. However, he didn't know how well the robot could hear, so he also decided to call 911 from a safer distance.

Moving very slowly and quietly, he wriggled out from under his bike gently and set it down. Then he rolled a bit farther away and held up his cell phone. Keeping his eyes on the robot, he moved his thumb over the phone's keypad.

The phone emitted a burst of light. Startled, Kevin dropped the phone in the dirt. He'd forgotten that he had been trying to set the phone on camera mode, and he realized he had just hit the flash. He blinked desperately, trying to clear the white spots from his sight and regain his night vision. He saw the robot whip its head around, its glowing blue eyes looking straight at him. Then the robot began marching toward Kevin, its huge legs bringing it ten feet closer with each step.

Kevin scrambled to his feet, accidentally kicking the phone away, and stumbled over to his bike. He looked up and saw a pair of headlights growing larger and brighter in the darkness. He realized the hum he'd noticed earlier hadn't been the robot, but a big black van that was coming straight at him—and fast. Kevin got the bike righted, stood up on the pedals, and tried to launch himself across the road.

He almost made it. The van skidded, its tires shrieking on the pavement, and then the van's bumper clipped Kevin's rear wheel from behind, knocking the bike into the air. He heard a loud crunch as he flew over the handlebars, and he reflexively closed his eyes as he sailed face-first into the ground.

This is gonna hurt.

A dull impact knocked the air out of Kevin's lungs. He'd hit something, but it didn't feel like the road, more like a metal bench. The pain wasn't nearly as bad as he'd thought it would be. He wondered if that meant he was hurt even worse than he'd feared. Then he felt the metal under him move and the air shift against the back of his neck. He opened his eyes.

He was clutched in the robot's metal fist. The robot was now kneeling, its insectlike face just two feet away from Kevin's, regarding him curiously through mechanical eyes. Kevin looked away and saw that the van, which now had a large dent in its side, had come to a stop and was parked sideways in the middle of the road.

"Put me down!" Kevin yanked at the metal fingers and kicked and twisted and wriggled as hard as he could. The robot opened its fingers, and Kevin fell the short distance to the ground. He rolled away from the robot and past the remains of his crushed bike, then leaped up and waved his arms at the van. Kevin yelled, "Help!"

The unseen driver sent the van into reverse, backing up fast along the road, then swung around in a tight, tire-squealing turn to race away from the abandoned farm. The black van quickly shot off into the night.

Kevin glanced back at the kneeling robot. It was peering after the van curiously. Hoping the driver would turn around, Kevin kept waving his arms until its taillights disappeared in the darkness. Then he heard a hum and a whirr behind him, and he froze, expecting some terrible weapon to appear in his face. But nothing happened. He risked looking back and saw that the robot was struggling to rise to its feet. The pistons in its lower left leg were bent. The robot looked at Kevin's ruined bike, then looked directly at Kevin himself.

"Are you undamaged, immature human?" the robot asked in a deep, booming voice. Every hair on Kevin's head felt like it was standing on end, as if he'd been electrocuted. Kevin was surprised that the robot spoke English. Then he relaxed, just a teeny tiny bit, when he began to realize why the robot had leaped across the road to pluck him out of the air. The robot had *saved his life* and, in doing so, had been hit by the van instead.

"I'm . . . okay," Kevin said cautiously. "You . . . you saved me?"

"The speeding vehicle would have killed you," the robot bellowed.

Kevin wasn't sure what to say next. They stood there in silence for a moment. Then he asked the obvious. "You speak English?"

"Yes."

Kevin thought about the battle in Mission City that had left his parents dead. The videos of that battle showed robots fighting one another, and he'd read that one group of robots was actually trying to protect humans from other robots. Despite the fact that the robot kneeling before him had taken a hit from a van to save his life, Kevin had no idea whether this particular robot could be trusted.

"Why did you save me? You, um, got hurt." He gestured to the robot's injured leg.

"Every life has value," the robot boomed. "What is your name?"

"You don't have to shout," Kevin said. "My name's Kevin. Kevin Bowman. What about your leg?"

The robot looked down at the straining pistons in his leg, then looked back at Kevin.

"I am repairable," he said. "My name is Gears."

In the van, a very rattled Simon Clay tried to stop hyperventilating as he headed north. He was driving just under the speed limit and kept looking in his rearview mirror to make sure he wasn't being followed.

It was only dumb luck that the kid hadn't been hurt or killed. He'd suddenly appeared out of nowhere! Clay prided himself on his extensive resources, but if he'd accidentally killed some idiot kid who shouldn't have been riding his bike at night, he doubted his resources were enough to make a legal problem like *that* go away.

As for the robot who had saved the kid, that was another problem entirely.

Clay was aware of the existence of Optimus Prime, the Autobot leader, and various details about Cybertronians. He had seen illegally obtained images of Optimus Prime's weapons officer, Ironhide, and the other Autobots who worked with NEST. He doubted it was a co-incidence that he'd literally run into a Cyber-tronian so soon after the raid. Had it tracked him somehow? He hadn't recognized it and wondered if it had been an Autobot or a Decep-ticon. Stealth Leader would want to know.

But there was no way Clay was going to turn around and drive back to get the information he knew his boss would crave. Clay had talked to enough huge, heavily armed robots for one night. Still, the questions nagged at him. And the more he thought about those questions, the more he realized that both Autobots and Decep-ticons now had ample reason to be hunting him down. And what about the police? He'd left the scene of a hit-and-run! What if the kid reported him?

Clay looked again in his rearview mirror. No one was behind the van. He switched on his radar detector and police scanner, and then he stepped on the gas.

Chapter Seven
IT TAKES TWO

Kevin's cell phone rang. He was still standing beside Gears on the ridge that overlooked the abandoned farm when he heard the familiar ringing noise. He reflexively reached into his pocket before he remembered he'd dropped the phone when the flash had gone off. Gears followed Kevin's gaze to the phone lying at the edge of the road, the screen lit up with the incoming call.

Gears lurched into action. Stepping shakily

into the road, he stood on his good leg as he lifted his damaged foot over the blinking phone. Seeing that Gears was about to bring his foot down, Kevin shouted, "No, wait! Gears! It's not a weapon! It's just a phone!"

Gears glanced at Kevin, then cautiously lowered his foot away from the phone. Kevin checked both ways for any more mysterious vehicles before he darted across the road and picked up the phone. Looking at the number, he saw the call was from his brother.

It wasn't unusual for Duane to check in on Kevin at night, and Kevin didn't want Duane to be worried about him. He also didn't think it would be a good idea to tell Duane that he was with a robot from outer space, because if the Army found out about Gears…Kevin could only imagine what would happen next. He looked at Gears and said, "Don't say a word."

Then he pressed a button on the phone as he stepped away from Gears and said as casually as he could, "Hey, Duane. What's up?"

Gears watched Kevin for a moment, then resumed his examination of his damaged leg. Seeing where the housing was bent around a piston, he raised his metal fist and began pounding at the housing, trying to put it back into its proper alignment.

Kevin, startled by the hammerlike clanging of metal on metal, nearly dropped the phone again. "What's that?" he repeated. "No! No, nothing's wrong. Gil and I are, uh... we're just watching a movie."

Gears wiggled his leg and wrenched the damaged metal away from the stuck piston, then began trying to bash out the dent.

CLANG! CLANG! CLANG!

"You're right, Duane," Kevin continued,

cupping a hand around his phone so he could hear better. "We do have it up way too loud! I'm sorry. Hey, Gilbert, could you turn that down?" Kevin waved his hand frantically at Gears.

Gears looked around and behind him, as if he might find someone or something named Gilbert. Seeing no one, Gears continued bashing away at his leg.

"Sorry, Duane!" Kevin yelled into the phone. "I don't know what's gotten into him tonight. Yeah, the science project's going okay. It's great, even! We'll talk about it tomorrow, okay? Duane? Duane?"

Kevin's brother's voice had dissolved in a burst of static, and then the connection broke. Kevin stared at the phone in bafflement, then noticed Gears had stopped his attempted repairs and was staring into the sky. Kevin looked up and saw another streak of light racing across the darkness.

"Another meteor!" Kevin said as he pocketed his phone. But then he noticed how Gears stiffened, and he added, "It's another robot, isn't it? Like you?"

"It is following the same trajectory," Gears said. "You should get out of sight, Kevin Bowman. Now!"

Kevin did not question the urgency in Gears's voice. He jumped away from Gears and took cover in a shallow ditch.

"Stay down!"

The meteor roared to Earth and slammed into the land behind the farmhouse. It ripped across the ground, leaving a flaming trail in its wake, before it came to rest about a hundred yards short of the crater left by Gears's own arrival.

Despite Gears's command to stay down, Kevin couldn't resist lifting his head to peer at the abandoned farm. A chrome robot crackling with red electric sparks rose from the smoking crater and turned his head to survey the terrain. His glowing red eyes gleamed in the dark.

"Reverb!" Gears bellowed, and the systems beneath his armored backplate began whirring madly.

Responding to Gears's voice, the chrome robot looked over at Gears and instantly charged. Kevin shrank back down into the ditch, but Gears thudded down the ridge and jumped over an old barbed-wire fence to confront the new arrival head-on. The two giants smashed into each other with a crunch of metal and locked arms. Gears thrust his right arm out, and Kevin watched in fascination as the arm's components smoothly rearranged themselves with a series of clicks into a cannon. But before Gears could take aim, Reverb grabbed the weapon, spinning Gears around and flinging him past the derelict SUV and into the shed that housed the rusted tractor. The shed exploded into thousands of splinters, sending the tractor rolling over onto its side and knocking the SUV off its cinder blocks.

Gears fired a burst of shots at Reverb, missing him and plowing holes in the parched grass. Reverb shrugged his shoulders, and a metal cone rose out of his armored chest. He flicked his sharp chin, and a huge thunderclap of noise filled the night. The sonic blast hit Gears in the chest, knocking him down flat and leaving him stunned.

Kevin was sprawled on the ground with his hands clamped over his ringing ears when he saw Gears go down. He felt powerless.

Reverb pounced on the fallen robot, his right hand re-forming into a nasty-looking spike as red indicator lights pulsed on his back. Gears, still woozy, managed to catch Reverb's wrist before he could drive the spike home and then swung his good leg up to kick Reverb, sending him crashing into the old farmhouse's porch. Gears climbed to his feet and advanced steadily, dragging his left leg slightly.

Reverb moved more quickly, snatching the barbed-wire fence that Gears had jumped over earlier. Reverb yanked several yards of wire from the earth, then whipped the wire at Gears, snaring a shoulder, and dodged left to wrap the fence around his opponent. Kevin's ears were still ringing, but he noticed that the lights on Reverb's back had changed from red to yellow.

Gears spun in the other direction, unwinding the barbed wire before it could bind and pin his upper arms. Reverb's backlights flashed yellow several times and then turned green. Seeing this, Kevin wasn't sure what Reverb was about to do, but he knew it couldn't be good. Kevin shouted, "Gears! Look out!"

Distracted by Kevin's voice, Reverb turned slightly as his chest-mounted sonic cannon engaged. Gears took advantage by throwing his body away from Reverb, just as Reverb's cannon launched a sonic wave that blew apart all that remained of the farmhouse.

Reverb was still scanning the area, searching for Gears's unseen ally, when Gears grabbed him and lifted him off the ground. Gears's damaged leg screeched as he lurched toward the rusted tractor that rested on its side amid the ruined pieces of the shed. In a raw display of strength, Gears body-slammed Reverb down upon the tractor. Reverb's legs kicked spasmodically at the impact, and panels popped open on his chest and legs.

Kevin heard a low electronic whine and saw Reverb's limbs go slack. Gears stepped back from the fallen robot, who was still twitching and emitting little bursts of sparks, then turned and made his way painfully back up the ridge.

Massaging his ears as he rose from his hiding place, Kevin whispered, "Did you kill it?"

"His name is *Reverb*," Gears said, apparently taking exception to the word *it*. "He is damaged. But because he is one of Megatron's most dedicated servants, his systems are likely booby-trapped. If I try to demolish him, I may be killed myself and fail to complete my mission."

Kevin shook his head. "Who's Megatron? And what's your mission?"

Ignoring Kevin's questions, Gears glanced back at Reverb. "We have to leave the area at once, Kevin Bowman. There may be more Decepticons coming, and I am not operating at peak efficiency. I will be at a disadvantage if there is another fight."

"*More* Decepticons?" Kevin said, exasperated. He knew from the news report that those were the robots who were supposedly behind all the attacks on humans. "Why?!"

Gears sighed. "Come with me. I will explain in transit. But first, I require a disguise." He looked back down the hill and studied the derelict SUV. He emitted a laser light grid, scanning it thoroughly. Then, to Kevin's astonishment, Gears began to change, his limbs folding in on themselves with a whine of spinning parts and telescoping pistons. Gears's metal parts were also changing color, shifting from shiny red, silver, and blue to a more dingy, rust-worn finish. Within seconds, Kevin was staring at an *exact* replica of the old SUV.

"Wow!" Kevin said. "That's amazing!"

"It's how my people blend in on your world," Gears said matter-of-factly, his voice rumbling out from under the battered hood. "We must go now." The exhaust coughed once at the back of the SUV, and then the engine roared to life. Despite Gears's changed appearance, the engine sounded remarkably powerful. The front passenger door popped open.

"Very impressive, Gears," Kevin said. "But you're forgetting something."

"What is that, Kevin Bowman?"

Kevin pointed to the SUV's bare, rusty axles. "We'll get farther if you make yourself some tires."

"I can do that," Gears said. A hissing sound

came from under the SUV, and then tires spiraled out and shifted into position on the axles.

Climbing into the front passenger seat and buckling in, Kevin said, "Shouldn't we notify the authorities about that guy Reverb?"

"I intercepted transmissions during my descent to Earth. I believe the authorities are already on their way."

Gears gunned his engine and zoomed down the dark road.

Chapter Eight
MISSION CONTROL

To Kevin's relief, Gears's imitation of the battered, old SUV hadn't extended to the internal systems. The engine hummed smoothly as they zoomed alongside the ridge, and the front seat was quite comfortable. However, even though Gears kept the car—or, rather, himself—on the road, Kevin did feel uneasy every time he glanced at the empty seat behind the steering wheel.

"So," Kevin said, "your people are robots who can turn into cars?"

"Not robots," came Gears's voice through the speaker system. "Robots are programmed and merely the sum of their metal and parts. We are autonomous organisms."

"Oh," Kevin said. "I didn't mean to offend you or anything."

"You have not offended me, Kevin Bowman."

"You can just call me Kevin. Now, can you explain this whole Decepticon thing? Why do they hate us so much?"

The SUV fishtailed slightly across the road before resuming its course. "Both Reverb and I are Cybertronians, beings from Cybertron. For centuries, two factions of our species have been locked in a civil war. Those known as the Decepticons seek the domination of others above all things. I am allied with the other faction, the Autobots. The Autobots build what Decepticons would destroy. We protect what they would exterminate."

"So...you're with the good guys."

Gears was silent for a moment, then replied, "Few beings think of themselves as evil. Many justify their actions as good, even if they are not. But if you believe the 'good guys' would not harm any life-form, then you may consider me as a member of that team."

"Okay. Intelligent robots, civil war, you're the good guys. Got it. So where are we going?"

"Not far," Gears said. "I will find a safe place to leave you, and then I will carry out my mission."

"What mission? What are you talking about?"

When Gears did not give an immediate response, Kevin thought he had decided to stop talking. But about thirty seconds later, Gears said, "I seek a munitions stronghold. I must get there before the Decepticons and secure what's inside. If the Decepticons were to get there first...it would be very bad for humans."

"Oh." Kevin thought about his parents. If Gears could stop something like that from happening again... "How fast can you get there? Where is it?"

"It is located approximately forty-five miles to the northeast of the town you call Hurley's Crossing."

Kevin's eyes went wide with surprise. "You mean the Hawthorne Army Depot! That's where my brother works!" Then he thought for a moment about what might happen if Decepticons attacked the base.... "Wait, I have to call him!"

"Your communications system won't work, Kevin."

Kevin checked his cell phone, but its screen

was blank. He jabbed at it with his fingers, but it refused to turn on. "It's fried," Kevin said. "How did you know?"

"I perceived a communications disruption just before Reverb landed. Reverb must have done it to protect himself during his insertion into your environment."

"But that didn't happen when *you* landed."

"Communications disruptions are one of Reverb's...specialties," Gears growled. "Where is your dwelling? Will you be safe there?"

"Oh no you don't. I'm coming with you. You *have* to bring me. I need to know if my brother is all right."

"No, Kevin. This mission is too dangerous for an immature human."

"Oh, yeah? Well, consider the fact that this 'immature human' just saved you from a Decepticon."

Gears swerved again. "I would have achieved a tactical advantage over Reverb in seven more seconds at most. Your distraction merely accelerated that process slightly."

"Really? I may not know much about Decepticons or Autobots or Cyber—uh, Cyber..."

"Cybertronians."

"...Cybertronians," Kevin echoed, trying to keep the names straight, "but it sure looked to me like he was about to clean your clock."

"Clean my clock?"

"You know... beat you up, win the fight, total smackdown."

"That is unlikely," Gears said stubbornly.

"Unlikely, but not impossible?"

Gears considered that. "Unlikely."

"Anyway, I'm not getting out of this car."

"I *am* this car, Kevin. You do not have a choice in the matter."

Fuming silently, Kevin looked out the window.

"There *is* an aspect of this mission where I require assistance," Gears said. "My navigational systems and magnetic sensors were damaged while fighting Reverb, and I did not have time to download information about your transportation infrastructure."

"Huh?"

"Please explain the meaning of 'huh.'"

"What are you talking about? Are you saying…you don't know the way?"

"That is correct," Gears admitted. "Do you?"

"Sure, I do."

"This is optimal. Once you tell me the ideal route, my mission may proceed."

Kevin looked out the window again.

"Kevin?"

"I heard you."

Sounding slightly flustered, Gears said, "You will not tell me the route?"

"No. But I'll show you."

As they headed up Route 95, Kevin pressed his head against the passenger door's window. It was odd to think that the glass, like every part of the car, was actually a part of Gears. Kevin stared at the stars.

Kevin said, "So you're from outer space?"

"Cybertronians do not call it that," Gears said. "But yes, I am from beyond your solar system."

"I was looking at the Great Bear earlier," Kevin said. "Do you know it?"

"No."

"It's a constellation." Kevin pointed through

the windshield. The Big Dipper hung over the mountains to the north, not far from Canis Major, the Great Dog. "And that's the Great Dog. It contains Sirius, the brightest star in the sky."

"I know that star," Gears said. "We call it..." He uttered a terrible electronic screeching and squalling sound.

"Wow," Kevin said. "I'll stick with *Sirius*."

"I have been there," Gears said.

"To Sirius? Really? What's it like?"

"It has one planet, which is now a radio-active battlefield," Gears said. "Nothing has been able to live there for nearly two thousand years."

"Oh," Kevin said. It was awful to think that the brightest star in the sky was no more immune to war than any other place. "How many worlds have you been to?"

"Seventy-four."

"And which was your favorite?"

"The orbital ring cities of Tharkoros VII are an admirable feat of engineering. But I would most like to see Cybertron, my home world, as it was before the war."

"Where is Cybertron?"

Several seconds passed before Gears replied, "It is not visible in your sky."

"Oh. So, Gears, what's your plan once we reach Hawthorne?"

"When we are near my destination, I shall leave the roadway and attempt to locate the site of the munitions stronghold. Before that, I shall find a safe place to leave you."

"But you said you can't navigate."

"Once I am close enough to the stronghold, I can use other methods."

Trying to think of some way to stick with

Gears, Kevin said, "But Gears…if what you said is true, that the 'authorities' are aware of you and Reverb landing in Nevada, then the Army will have set up checkpoints even before you get to Hawthorne. Trust me on this, Army soldiers will find an empty car driving itself more than a little suspicious."

Gears considered this information, then said, "I can generate a hologram of a human driver."

"The soldiers will question the driver. Does your hologram already know all the answers to those questions?"

"I don't know. What are the questions?"

Kevin laughed. "You don't know *anything* about the Army base, or Hawthorne, or even Nevada. But hey, I have an idea! What if you put the hologram directly over me, like a costume I could wear?"

"Well," Gears mused, "I *could* scan your body

and project a hologram around you. I could probably make the hologram follow your movements. I understand what you are proposing, Kevin, but...it is too dangerous."

"Got any better ideas? You *do* need to complete your mission, right?"

Gears thought in silence as the highway markers whizzed by. At last, he said, "This is a war, Kevin. And in war, things are very different from what you may imagine. Battles may seem glorious and heroic to the young, but they are not. In war, innocent people die for no reason other than being in the wrong place at the wrong time."

"I know that, Gears," Kevin said as he stared out the window. "Believe me. I know."

Chapter Nine
CRIME SCENE INVESTIGATION

The large black NEST helicopter hovered over the abandoned farm on the outskirts of Hurley's Crossing where a pair of "meteorites" had left two long furrows in the ground. The helicopter landed, and then the cargo doors opened. Bumblebee and Ratchet hopped out with cannons ready, followed by a squad of soldiers, and they surveyed the farm's ruined structures. When no opposition presented itself, the Autobots and humans lowered their weapons.

While the soldiers fanned out, Bumblebee sought an appropriate song from the airwaves to convey his dilemma. Seconds later, he startled the soldiers when he emitted a female voice that sang, "*Where has everybody gone?*"

"Careful, Bumblebee," Ratchet teased. "You're disturbing the humans."

A soldier called out, "You two are going to want to see this."

Bumblebee and Ratchet followed the soldier and found a chrome-plated Cybertronian lying inert on the crumpled tractor. "Is it dead?" the soldier asked.

"He is alive but damaged," Ratchet said. Extending his arm, Ratchet dragged a metal finger across the emblem on the unconscious Cybertronian's chrome chest. Both Ratchet and Bumblebee had seen the emblem far too many times, over centuries of war. "And he is a Decepticon," Ratchet added. "Secure him for revival and interrogation."

The NEST commandos began securing the new arrival. Ratchet had learned not to underestimate humans' bravery and capabilities, but as he looked at the Decepticon, he knew without a doubt that he had not been knocked out by a human. Ratchet was certain it had been another Cybertronian, probably an Autobot. He looked at Bumblebee and knew his friend was thinking the same thing. Bumblebee walked off, heading for the nearby road that passed the farm.

Looking around, Ratchet noticed the derelict, wheel-less SUV that appeared to have fallen off its cinder blocks. He couldn't imagine an Autobot would have chosen such a piece of junk as a disguise.

He looked for Bumblebee and saw him standing by the road, a bicycle dangling from one hand. *A child's bike*, Ratchet thought. The bike's back end was twisted, the wheel hanging from a crushed length of chain.

Climbing the slope to the roadway to see what else Bumblebee had found, Ratchet heard shouts behind him. Glancing back, he saw that the chrome Decepticon had sat up and started to struggle with the soldiers. The Decepticon was having trouble getting his damaged limbs to obey his commands.

Ratchet saw that the NEST commandos had been trying to bind the Decepticon's hands with oversize magnetic cuffs and suspected that they had accidentally awakened him. One cuff was closed around the Decepticon's thick left wrist, but the other swung open uselessly near his right wrist.

The Decepticon flung a soldier aside, then whirled to face the rest of the squad. The soldiers backed away, aiming their rifles at their attacker. Ratchet leaped down the hill and landed between the Decepticon and the soldiers, then ducked as Bumblebee soared overhead, dropping the bicycle as he aimed a flying tackle at the Decepticon.

It was a foolhardy move, as Ratchet might have warned his friend. The Decepticon caught Bumblebee's arm, using the Autobot's own momentum against him, and hurled him over the ruins of the house. Ratchet, seeing an opening, charged the Decepticon and hit him in his armored midsection, slamming him to the ground and then collapsing on top of him. The Decepticon thrashed wildly, but Ratchet held on.

"Stay back," Ratchet commanded the soldiers. He was having some difficulty pinning the Decepticon, but his action had bought time for Bumblebee to rejoin the fight. Bumblebee grabbed the Decepticon's legs, which only made the Decepticon struggle more frantically.

"Stop," Ratchet said. "You are beaten. Don't make the humans use carbon-fiber restraints on you. I am told it is extremely painful."

Apparently accepting that he was no match for two Autobots, the Decepticon stopped struggling. "Please let me up," he said meekly. "After I arrived, when I resumed full functionality, I was attacked by humans. It frightened me. I reacted instinctively."

"You are a Decepticon," Ratchet said.

"I am a defector!"

Bumblebee responded with an electronic raspberry, then dipped into his own library of pop music and sounded, *"Liar, liar, pants on fire."*

"I speak the truth!" the Decepticon insisted. "My name is Reverb. I am part of a secret movement that has rejected Megatron's leadership.

Megatron has brought us nothing but war. We seek to overthrow him. We work for peace. There are only a few of us, but our numbers are growing. And we need your help."

Ratchet had never heard of Reverb. But there were many new Cybertronians coming to Earth, both Autobots and Decepticons, and the Cybertronians' civil war had spread to many planets. The Autobots had tried for years to persuade the Decepticons to reject Megatron's rule. If any were doing so, it could bring their terrible war closer to a peaceful end.

"You will be restrained," Ratchet told Reverb. "The magnetic cuffs will cut the power to your weapons and make it difficult for you to change form. I promise it is not painful. After you are restrained, my allies and I will listen to your story."

"Thank you," Reverb said. He made no

attempt to resist as Ratchet fitted the dangling cuff over his other wrist and activated the restraints' magnetic field. The two Autobots helped Reverb to his feet and kept their own hands clamped to his upper arms.

"Now," said Ratchet, "tell us what happened after you arrived."

"I am in pursuit of another Decepticon, one loyal to Megatron. His mission is to destroy a munitions stronghold near here. I must stop him."

The two Autobots exchanged a glance. They both suspected that Reverb was referring to the Hawthorne Army Depot. Aiming a thumb at the two long furrows that cut into the farmland, Ratchet faced Reverb and said, "What happened to the other Decepticon?"

"He arrived just before I did. We fought." Reverb looked at the twisted bicycle that lay nearby. "I was about to defeat him when I heard a human child cry out, up there on the roadway. I thought the child might be in danger and turned to look. When I did so, Megatron's agent took advantage of my distraction."

"Did you see the child?"

"No."

Ratchet looked again to Bumblebee, who shrugged his shoulders. Although the Decepticon's story sounded plausible, the Autobots knew that Decepticons were notoriously convincing liars. Turning to face the NEST technician, Ratchet said, "Contact Hawthorne."

The tech spoke into his headset, then waited for a response. He looked back at the Autobots and said with alarm, "No answer. All communications in the area have been knocked out. It's like there's a transmissions blackout over Nevada...maybe even beyond Nevada."

Facing Bumblebee, Ratchet tried transmitting a private communications burst, one with very limited range. *"Bumblebee, do you read this?"*

Bumblebee nodded and sent back, *"I hear you fine, but I'm not picking up any long-range transmissions."* He looked back at Reverb.

"My opponent must have disrupted communications," Reverb said, then added wistfully, "I wish I knew what happened to the child. You did not find it?"

"No, just a broken bicycle," Ratchet replied.

"Perhaps my opponent took the child as a prisoner." Reverb shifted anxiously on his feet. "You must not let any Decepticon reach the munitions stronghold!"

Ratchet believed Optimus Prime would have known what to do next and wished the Autobot leader were around to consult. Without any operating long-range communications systems, contacting Optimus was impossible, at least for the moment. Someone had to make a decision. "We will fly to Hawthorne," Ratchet declared, "and see if we can find any sign of the other Decepticon and the missing child." He signaled to the NEST team to move out. "You will stay restrained, Reverb, at least for now."

Bumblebee began to protest, clearly upset that Reverb was coming at all. But Ratchet cut his friend's objections off with a curt wave of his hand. This was not the time to argue.

"I will do anything you ask," Reverb said. "Just let me help you. We must stop my enemy from causing any more harm.

"He is a liar and a killer. His name is Gears."

Chapter Ten

TRAFFIC JAM

Still traveling under the stars in his battered-SUV mode, Gears carried Kevin over a stretch of the Veterans Memorial Highway that snaked through a mountain pass, heading toward the town of Hawthorne, Nevada. As they rounded a bend in the highway, they saw the lights of the base in the distance. The town was virtually surrounded by the Hawthorne Army Depot, which consisted of a web of roads linking bunkers and testing grounds that sprawled across the desert. Signs warned travelers not to leave the road because of the danger posed by unexploded munitions left over from decades of Army testing.

"Uh-oh," Kevin said as he saw a long line of taillights ahead.

Gears said, "Is there an automobile accident in front of us?"

"No. A roadblock."

Gears slowed to a stop behind the car in front of them. Kevin unbuckled his seat belt, scooted over quickly to get behind the steering wheel, and buckled himself into the driver's seat. He tried to look casual, as if twelve-year-olds drove all the time. When traffic started moving, Gears edged forward until Kevin could see the armed soldiers up ahead, shining their flashlights into car windows.

"Do it now," Kevin said. "Do the hologram thing."

"Very well," Gears said. "I will make you look like a soldier."

"No! That won't work. They'll ask for an ID!"

They rolled forward a few feet. The soldiers were now just several cars ahead. Gears said, "What if I make you appear to be an officer?"

"It won't matter without ID," Kevin insisted. "And I don't know the base well enough to answer their questions correctly."

"We should have discussed this before," Gears said as they rolled forward again.

"It's too late! Make me a man."

"What does that mean?"

Kevin saw a soldier walking toward them, flashlight held loosely in one hand. "An *older* version of me!" Kevin blurted out. "Quick!"

He glanced in the mirror mounted outside the driver-side window. The mirror reflected the wrinkled face of an old man with a wild white beard covering his chin. "Not *that* old!" Kevin protested. "Make me five or six years older...a teenager!"

Kevin heard the soldier's boots on the gravel and saw the beam from the flashlight traveling closer. He rolled down the window as the soldier stepped to his door.

"That's funny," the soldier said, blinking his eyes. "A moment ago, you looked...different." He played the light across the passenger seat as he looked around the cab.

Kevin's heart hammered in his chest as he lowered his voice and said, "Different? What do you mean?"

"Never mind," the soldier said, shaking his head. "Must've been the lights reflected on your windshield. This area is closed to all nonessential traffic."

"But...I have to see my brother. He works at the depot."

"We're on lockdown, along with about half of Nevada," the soldier said. "No visitors."

Thinking fast, Kevin said, "But I'm not going to the depot itself. My brother and I are supposed to meet in town."

The soldier gave Kevin a skeptical look. Kevin wondered how long Gears could maintain the hologram that concealed his true appearance. The soldier said, "Sorry, son, but you'll have to move along to the—"

"Listen, I drove up from Hurley's Crossing," Kevin said desperately. "I saw two giant robots fighting, not far from my house!"

The soldier lifted his eyebrows. "Giant robots?"

"I swear, it's true! I called my brother and he told me to come at once, that it would be safer here. That was the last thing he said before my phone got fried."

The soldier looked at the car that was waiting behind Kevin, then asked, "Who's your brother?"

Kevin took a deep breath. "Sergeant Duane Bowman."

"And what's your name?"

"Kevin Bowman."

"Let me see your license."

"I don't have it," Kevin said. "I left my wallet at home. When I saw the robots, I just ran for the car."

The soldier's flashlight beam flicked over Kevin's face. The soldier said, "How old are you?"

"Seventeen," Kevin said, hoping Gears hadn't created a hologram that looked twice that age. Just to be safe, he added, "Almost eighteen." He held his breath.

"Communications are out," the soldier said, "so I can't contact your brother for you. But I'll let you proceed to base HQ." He reached into a pocket, pulled out an orange piece of paper, and held it out to Kevin. "You go straight to the address on that pass, and you tell the people there what you told me about the robots." Gears was able to make the hologram's arm move with Kevin's so he could grasp the pass.

"Yes, sir, I'll do that," Kevin said, finally able to exhale. "Thank you."

Stepping back from the SUV, the soldier motioned for Kevin to steer into an empty lane alongside the roadblock. The soldier said, "While you're in Hawthorne, you might consider getting a new car. This one looks beyond ready for the graveyard."

The SUV's engine snarled. Kevin tapped the

dashboard and said, "You wouldn't believe what's under the hood."

As they pulled into the other lane and away from the soldier, Kevin glanced in the rearview mirror and saw the hologram that Gears was still generating. "You gave me long curly hair and a mustache?!"

"It was a successful ruse, was it not?" Gears said as he deactivated the hologram.

"I guess." Kevin looked at the orange pass the soldier had given him and said, "And now we have direct access to the base. C'mon, let's move a little faster!"

Gears accelerated.

Aboard the NEST helicopter that had left the outskirts of Hurley's Crossing and was now heading for Hawthorne, soldiers kept watch over Reverb, who stood silently with his wrists secured by glowing manacles. Meanwhile, Bumblebee and Ratchet transmitted private short-range communications bursts to each other.

"*He is lying,*" Bumblebee insisted. "*You should have let me finish him. Instead we're taking this Decepticon right to the middle of an Army depot.*"

"*Finish him?*" Ratchet retorted. "*He nearly finished you!*"

"*I had him right where I wanted him,*" Bumblebee grumbled. "*But never mind that. Do you really believe him? Blaming some other Decepticon who just happened to have run away before we got there? Come on! He's the liar, Ratchet. And for all we know, he's the killer!*"

"*He sounds sincere. And in the meantime, he has not resisted us.*"

"That's because he's suckered you into taking him where he wants to go!"

Ratchet glanced at the chrome-plated Decepticon, whose lights in his armored back blinked green. *"If there is division in the Decepticons' ranks,"* Ratchet transmitted, *"we need to encourage it."*

Bumblebee shook his head. *"You're dreaming."*

"If so, it is a good dream. It's worth seeing if it can come true. I am tired of war, my friend. This conflict must stop."

Bumblebee sighed. *"I'm tired of war, too, Ratchet. But I don't want it to end because we lost."*

Chapter Eleven
COMMUNICATIONS ARE DOWN

In a warehouse at the Nevada Test and Training Range air base where Optimus Prime and Ironhide had defeated the three Decepticons, Optimus and Ironhide stood before a group of Army officers who were seated behind a long table. The Autobots had been answering their questions for more than an hour. Optimus Prime looked as patient as ever, but as the questions began to sound increasingly similar, Ironhide started fretting that they'd be answering the same questions for another hour or more.

A young, nervous-looking aide entered the warehouse through a heavy steel door and approached the table where the assembled officers sat. He came to a stop and stood at attention. The officers glanced over at him.

"What is it, Corporal?" asked one, a white-haired man whose uniform was covered with so many medals that he reminded Ironhide of an overly decorated Christmas tree that he'd seen once near Edwards Air Force Base. He did not understand why humans insisted on decorating trees.

The aide said, "Colonel Barnes would like to speak with you, General Marcus."

The general looked baffled for a moment, then annoyed. Ironhide had learned that was a normal reaction for humans who considered themselves too important and too busy to be bothered by anyone else.

"Then why doesn't Colonel Barnes use the telephone?" the general asked, his blue eyes narrowing. "This line is secure."

"Colonel Barnes is here in person, General Marcus," the aide said. He looked even more nervous as his eyes jumped to the two hulking Autobots.

General Marcus scowled as he rose from his chair. "I'll be right back." The aide followed him out of the room.

Ironhide looked at Optimus Prime, then transmitted a private short-range burst to ask, "*What are they doin', boss?*"

"*They don't want us to hear their discussion,*" Optimus transmitted in response.

"*They don't trust us? After everything we've done to help them?*"

"*Apparently not. Calm yourself, Ironhide. If we need to, we will ask General Marcus what was discussed.*"

"*And if he doesn't tell us?*"

"*This room's walls are made of aggregate stone reinforced with iron. Human auditory sensors are not powerful enough to hear voices through it. But mine can.*"

"*So, right now, you're listening to what they're saying?*" Ironhide asked.

"*I am not monitoring the general's conversation. That would be impolite.*"

"*Impolite?*" Ironhide shook his head with dismay. "*Personally, I'd like to know what they're saying.*"

"*But I am recording the conversation,*" Optimus continued. "*I will play it back if necessary.*" And then Optimus Prime did something he did not do often. He smiled.

General Marcus reentered the warehouse room, the heavy steel door shutting behind him. He returned to his seat beside the other officers. "We have a situation," he said. "About two hours ago, two meteoroids—"

"Excuse me, General Marcus," interrupted one of the other officers, an old, distinguished-looking human whose uniform was also covered with many colored bars and badges and ribbons.

"Yes, General Wichenstein?"

"This briefing should be limited to those with the proper clearance."

Before General Marcus could respond, Optimus Prime took one heavy step forward. The boom of the Autobot's metal foot resounded in the warehouse, and every officer turned to look up at him. Way up.

"We have a common enemy," Optimus Prime

said gravely. "And my people have died defending your world. It would be helpful if you treated us as your allies."

"And we sincerely appreciate and honor your people's sacrifice," General Wichenstein said. "We agreed to establish the NEST program so that our two species could work together against the Decepticon threat. But even allies have secrets they need to keep to themselves. As a military leader yourself, surely you understand this."

Outraged and making no effort to modulate the volume of his voice, Ironhide lurched forward and bellowed, "The Decepticons are up to something! We need to be out there blasting them, not standing around while you sit there flapping your jaws and leaking lubricant! Now tell us what's going on!"

General Camden laced his fingers together

before him, then said calmly, "You lack the necessary security clearance for that information."

"Security clearance?! I'll show you my security clearance—!"

"Ironhide, control yourself," Optimus said. Facing the officers, he continued, "The Decepticons have exterminated many worlds that were once green and beautiful, like yours. We have every reason to believe they intend to lay waste and destroy all life on Earth. Any knowledge we keep from each other gives them an advantage in this war, and gives the Decepticons a greater chance to accomplish their goals."

General Wichenstein started to respond, but General Marcus spoke first. "About two hours ago, two meteoroids entered Earth's atmosphere and crashed near the town of Hurley's Crossing, Nevada. For security's sake, we assumed the meteoroids were Cybertronians."

"We were already aware of the meteoroids," Optimus Prime said, "and assumed the same. NEST dispatched soldiers and our allies Bumblebee and Ratchet to the impact site. We are still waiting for their report."

"It might be a long wait," General Marcus said. "There has been a communications disruption across all channels. We suspect the meteoroids—uh, Cybertronians—caused the disruption."

Optimus Prime and Ironhide looked at each other. Optimus said, "Any disruption related to the landing should have ended by now."

"This one hasn't," General Marcus said. "Something in central Nevada is jamming communications for the entire western United States. We don't know what's causing it, nor can we determine the exact location of the jammer. We have placed all facilities on lockdown in anticipation of a possible attack, even though we have no idea where an attack might come from. In other words, gentlemen, we are blind."

General Wichenstein cleared his throat and said, "Area Fifty-One has to be the target. The Decepticons can't be allowed to capture the technology we have there."

"Area Fifty-One?" said another officer with disbelief, and then the officers began to argue.

The Autobots were aware of Area 51, the paradoxically best-known and yet most highly classified military base in the Nevada Test and Training Range. Also known as Dreamland, Paradise Ranch, and Homey Airport, Area 51 was reportedly where the Air Force secretly developed and tested new aircraft and weapons. Area 51 also had a long and popular association with UFO and conspiracy theorists.

Ironhide looked at Optimus Prime. Optimus shook his head.

"Area Fifty-One is not the Decepticons' target," Optimus Prime said, his rumbling voice silencing the quarreling officers instantly. Gesturing to the warehouse's walls, Optimus added, "Nor is this facility."

General Wichenstein said, "Are you forgetting they already attacked our perimeter tonight?"

"I am not dismissing the attack," Optimus Prime said. "Merely noting that the attack was not meant to gain control of this location."

"Then why *did* the Decepticons attack?" General Marcus asked.

"It was a feint," Optimus Prime said. "A decoy. It was designed to bring our forces here and keep us distracted. The true target is elsewhere. Is there a map of this area we can examine together?"

Aides scrambled to set up a projector and connect it to a laptop. Optimus Prime waited patiently until a map of Nevada was projected onto a wall. An aide quickly marked Hurley's Crossing and the Nevada Test and Training Range with red dots.

"We are southeast of Hurley's Crossing," Optimus Prime said. "What military facilities are north of there?"

"The Hawthorne Army Depot," General Marcus said.

"It's a storage area for munitions and explosives," General Wichenstein added. "Bombs, rockets, artillery shells—"

"That's basic stuff," Ironhide interrupted. "It's not technology the Decepticons would want."

Optimus Prime said, "Is there anything else

at the Hawthorne Army Depot? Something not publicly known?"

The generals looked at each other. That was all the answer Optimus Prime needed. He said, "We will prepare the NEST copter for immediate liftoff. Our destination is the Hawthorne Army Depot." Pausing to direct his gaze at General Marcus, he added, "I propose a joint mission, General."

General Marcus rose from the table and saluted the Autobot. "It would be an honor, Optimus Prime."

Chapter Twelve
STARLIGHT, STAR BRIGHT

Still in his rusted-SUV mode, Gears carried Kevin past the roadblock and the line of cars that were starting to back up on the opposite side of the highway.

"Hey! You missed the turn for the base!" said Kevin, who was still behind the steering wheel.

"I am not making that turn, Kevin," Gears replied. He continued driving until traffic had thinned out and then shut off his headlights and slowed, pulling off the road and onto loose gravel.

"What are you doing?" Kevin said. "We're not anywhere near base headquarters."

"I am not going to base headquarters," Gears said. "My mission lies elsewhere."

"But you said—"

"I am near my destination, Kevin. But I will have to cross restricted terrain to reach it." Gears opened the door. "Please get out. It would be unsafe for you to remain seated while I change form."

Kevin unlatched his seat belt and stepped out onto the side of the road. The night air was chilly, and Kevin shivered. With a whirring of pistons and a clattering of panels and parts, the SUV began to turn itself inside out.

"Hurry up, Gears. Another car will be coming soon."

Gears quickly resumed his robotic configuration, only now his metal plating retained the rusted color and texture of the SUV. "You must stay here, Kevin. It is only a matter of time before soldiers will pass here in a military vehicle. They will pick you up and take you to your brother." Gears looked away from Kevin, his glowing eyes surveying the bleak landscape.

"Oh," Kevin said, and was surprised to feel dismayed that his adventure with Gears was about to come to an end. "But...how do you know you're close to your destination? Are your navigational systems working again?"

"Not entirely. I still cannot access data about your transportation infrastructure. But my terrain sensors are functional, and I know we are nearly forty-five miles to the northeast of Hurley's Crossing and within walking distance of my destination. I will know the place when I find it." Gears looked down at him. "Good-bye, Kevin. You are a brave young human. I hope we meet again when my mission is complete."

Leaving Kevin at the edge of the road, Gears started to limp across the desert. Kevin called out, "Does it matter to you that you're walking the wrong way?"

Gears stopped and glanced back at the boy. "What do you mean?"

Kevin left the road, walked toward Gears, then headed off to the left and kept walking. Behind him, he heard Gears's powerful leg motors activate with a whine. A moment later, the Autobot shuffled in front of him. Gears said, "Where are you going, Kevin?"

"Northeast," Kevin answered, walking around Gears and continuing beneath the stars.

Gears moved after Kevin again. Every other step he took produced a screech followed by a mechanical groan. "My question did not concern a directional heading, Kevin," Gears said.

Kevin stopped short and turned to face Gears. "I know which way northeast is. You don't. Without me, you'll just wander around out here. You don't have time for that, do you?"

"You are not carrying a compass, Kevin," Gears said. "You do not know which way is north by northeast."

"Yes, I do." Kevin pointed upward. Gears craned his mechanical neck back to gaze at the stars that filled the night sky.

"I know about stars, remember? I can use them to navigate."

"Using the patterns you call constellations?"

"That's right. They tell me which way is northeast."

Gears looked back and forth across the sky. "Which constellations tell you this?"

Suspecting that Gears was hoping he would point out specific stars, Kevin stuck his hands in his pockets and rocked back on his feet. "Well, right now, Cygnus, the Swan, is just rising, and its right wing is above the horizon. Vega is to the east, in Lyra. Within an hour or so, the Swan's body will be visible, with the bright star Deneb in its tail. Then about an hour after that, the third star of the Summer Triangle, Altair, will appear, in Aquila the Eagle...."

"How do I know you are not just inventing these names of constellations? Or that any of them direct you to the northeast?"

"I got you this far, didn't I?"

Gears sighed. "Reverb must have damaged my compass, too. I wish I had placed this information into my programming module as a backup to my navigational systems. I will do so for future missions. Will you tell me which of your constellations indicates the northeast?"

"No," Kevin said with a smile. "You'll just have to follow me."

"You are behaving irrationally, Kevin. You saw the warning signs at Hawthorne. There may be unexploded munitions in this area. There is the possibility of encountering military personnel. And there may be Decepticons seeking to counter my mission. Each of these factors is very dangerous."

"You worry too much, Gears. Anybody ever tell you that?"

"I have properly calculated the risk factors, and—"

"The whole *night* has been dangerous!" Kevin said. "Where would I be safer than with you? You're a giant robo—um, Autobot!" He started walking. Gears shuffled after him.

They walked without talking for a while, Kevin's shoes crunching the dirt and Gears's heavy footfalls thumping up clouds of dust. Then Gears asked, "Is astral navigation a standard part of your academy training?"

"You mean, did I learn it in school?"

Gears took a moment to process Kevin's question, then said, "Yes. That is what I meant."

"No. Nobody learns stuff like that anymore. My mother taught me and Duane. She wanted to be an astronomer when she was young. She went into the Army instead. But she never stopped looking at the stars. She loved them, and she wanted us to love them, too."

"I am sorry, Kevin. Your mother must be worried about your safety. Is she at your dwelling now? With your father?"

"No," Kevin said. "She's dead. They both are."

Surprised, Gears paused in his tracks. Kevin

kept walking, trying to blink away tears. They started at the most unexpected times. He told himself to cut it out, that he wouldn't be able to see the stars if everything looked blurry. But really, he didn't want Gears to see him cry.

"I am sorry for your loss, Kevin. Was there an accident?"

"You could call it that."

Gears said nothing. And then Kevin began telling the story. How his parents had gone to Mission City and never returned. How the officers had come to their house with the news. How the government was forced to admit the almost unbelievable truth about alien robots.

"They must have been Decepticons," Kevin continued. "And if it weren't for them coming to Earth, my parents would probably still be alive. And my brother and I wouldn't be alone."

Gears came to an abrupt stop. "I am sorry, Kevin."

"It's not *your* fault," Kevin said, stopping in front of Gears. "You weren't even on Earth at the time."

Gears looked up at the stars, then lowered his head. "I do not know how your parents died, Kevin. But I assure you that the Autobots did not bring the Cybertron war to Earth. As I told you earlier, we came to Earth to *protect* life-forms from the Decepticons." Looking at Kevin, he continued, "I have lost many friends in this war. Some of them had their Sparks extinguished centuries ago, on worlds many light-years from this one, far from their homes."

Confused, Kevin asked, "Sparks?"

"The energy that gives us life," Gears explained. "Other losses are more recent. The

Decepticon I fought tonight, Reverb...he murdered my friend Tailgate ten years ago."

Kevin kicked at the ground. "Do you miss your friends? *Can* you miss them? Or are you like a big computer that doesn't review data again unless you have to?"

"I miss them, Kevin," Gears said. "I think about them often."

"Does that help?"

"It is strange," Gears said, returning his gaze to the stars. "Thinking about absent friends makes me sad that they are gone. But remembering them makes me happy, too. Perhaps my memories keep some aspect of them alive." He looked back down at Kevin. "We should keep walking."

"Okay," Kevin said. "This way." He started walking again. Gears followed, his motors thrumming while his damaged leg groaned. Kevin said, "You must hate the Decepticons, right? I mean, Reverb killed your friend Tail-gate. Do you hate him for it?"

Gears considered the question, then replied, "I have learned that hatred is a dangerous thing. To begin to hate is easy, but to stop is very hard. I will fight Decepticons and extinguish their Sparks if I have to. But not because I hate them. I will do it because if I do not, then they will destroy others and cause much misery for those who survive and—" Gears stopped again and turned slightly to his right.

"Gears? What is it?"

"My sensors are picking up readings."

"What kind of readings? Are we near your destination?"

"No," Gears said. "This is something else. Two objects, on the ground, approaching at high speed. Please move behind me, Kevin. We are about to be attacked."

Chapter Thirteen
TANK ATTACK

Kevin stepped quickly behind Gears's uninjured leg. Gears's metal arms whirred and clattered, changing into cannons.

"They are not Decepticons," Gears said. "I know because they are headed right for us instead of trying to flank us."

Kevin heard a low-pitched whine, engines approaching their position from somewhere in front of Gears.

"A thousand meters," Gears announced calmly.

Kevin saw a burst of fire in the darkness. A moment later Kevin heard a loud *boom*.

"Lie flat, Kevin," Gears said, and his cannon spat a flame. A split second later, a shell exploded in the air overhead, lighting up the night.

Kevin felt a blast of heat against his face. Squinting his eyes, he said, "Who's shooting at us?"

"Tanks," Gears said. "Manufactured by humans, but I sense no life-forms. They are remote-controlled. You should take cover."

Good idea, thought Kevin as he looked around the flat desert plain, but... "There is no cover!"

As the tanks drew closer, Gears knelt down, lowered his head, and said, "Climb onto my shoulder and hold on tight."

The thrum of the tanks' engines had risen to a loud whine. Kevin scrambled up Gears's arm, his feet slipping and sliding on the smooth metal armor. Gears's armor was surprisingly warm to the touch. Kevin's fingers gripped the edge of the armor plate protecting Gears's neck and held on as Gears stood back up.

"Do not touch the heat exchangers on my backplate," Gears warned. "They get very hot."

"Heat exchangers? Um, okaaaaay. As soon as I figure out what they are, I won't touch them. Anything else you want to tell me?"

"Do not fall off."

Gears began moving with long strides, his left leg still dragging a bit. Kevin could see the tanks now. They were low, bulbous shapes prowling the night like predators. One tank opened fire with a rat-a-tat of guns. Without slowing his pace, Gears threw his arm up in front of him. Kevin saw a bright flash and heard the rattle of bullets bouncing off Gears's raised arm.

Kevin shouted, "Are you hurt?"

"Their antipersonnel weapons cannot penetrate my armor. But it is not a pleasant sensation."

Boom!

"Hold on!" Gears said, and then he leaped forward. Kevin's head snapped back as the great metal body left the ground. Kevin closed his eyes and held on tight to the edge of the shoulder armor.

The fired shell burst behind them, and the shock wave threw Gears forward. Heat washed over Kevin's back, and little rocks and clumps of dirt rained down on them, but Gears twisted his body in the air and landed on his feet. Kevin grunted with the impact.

Gears said, "Are you all right?"

"Oh yeah, just great!" Kevin gasped. "Get us out of here!"

"I need to get closer to them."

"Closer?!"

Gears didn't answer. He turned with Kevin still on his shoulder and began to run across the desert, his shoulder lurching each time he came down heavily on his damaged leg. He raised his arm and fired his weapon.

Flames burst around them and Kevin saw the two tanks ahead. "Gears! You're going to run right between them!"

"Yes," Gears said. "I am."

One of the pistons in his damaged leg gave a screech. Gears stumbled, then fell to one knee, but lifted his torso fast to protect the boy on his back. One tank opened fire with a machine gun, and bullets bounced off Gears's chest plate as he got up and resumed his fast lope across the plain. Kevin managed to hold on despite the bone-jarring roller-coaster ride, but when they were nearing the area between the robot tanks, he yelled, "This was a bad idea!"

Then Gears stopped and squatted low to the ground, his damaged leg making an awful grinding sound. On either side of him, the tanks elevated their turrets and repositioned their guns. Kevin's eyes went wide with fear as he clung tighter to Gears, and then the tank to their left fired.

Gears sprang high into the air. The tank's fired missile zoomed below his body at the same time that the second tank fired. Gears and Kevin were still airborne as Gears rapidly calculated that the first tank's missile would strike the second tank, and that the second tank's missile would pass under him and fly over the first tank. In midair, he smashed his fist into the side of the second tank's missile, altering its trajectory.

The first missile struck the second tank,

blowing it to bits, and then the other missile went straight into the first tank, causing another explosion.

Gears landed on his good leg, but the power of the blasts knocked him off balance, and Kevin flew from his shoulders. Kevin and Gears rolled across the ground, and when they looked back at the tanks, they saw nothing but burning, shredded metal.

"Are you all right, Kevin?"

"That was crazy," Kevin said, trying to catch his breath. "Are *you* all right?"

"Except for my damaged leg, I am fully functional." Gears got to his feet, eyes scanning the desert.

"Gears, those were Army tanks. They might send more. We can't stay here."

"We are within two thousand feet of my destination," Gears said.

"How do you know?"

Gears tapped his metal chest. "My proximity locator just activated. I can feel it."

"Proximity locator?"

"It is very old and durable Cybertronian technology. Reverb's communications disruption does not affect it."

"Oh," Kevin said. "So, which way from here?"

"That way," Gears said. He pointed to a low, rocky hill sticking up above the flat plain. "That hill conceals the munitions."

Kevin looked at the rocky hill. Behind it, in the sky, Cygnus had risen. "But I don't see anything. If it is there, how do we know it's not rigged with traps or something?"

Gears began to limp forward again. "It is underground. It has no defenses. It is a very old facility."

"How old?" Thinking back to what he knew

about Hawthorne, he said, "My brother said the depot opened in … 1930, I think."

"Older than that," Gears said. "This munitions stronghold was first established over nineteen thousand years ago."

"What? Gears, that … that's impossible! There weren't even humans here then."

"I did not say the stronghold was established by humans."

They arrived at the base of the rocky hill. Gears reached out to touch a rough wall of rock, his metal fingers searching for something. Dirt crumbled around his hand as he found and reached into a dark recess. A crack appeared at the top of the wall, widening to the left and right, then zipping in perfect straight lines down to the desert floor. A rectangle of white light began to glow, emanating from within the hill. Kevin heard a low rumble as the rocky wall began to shift. Chunks of small stones bounced down the wall's surface, and then dust billowed out from the opening. He turned his face away from the intensifying glow and the cloud of silt that fell over them.

When Kevin looked back, the light had faded and a massive doorway yawned in the side of the rocky hill. "What is this place?" he asked in astonishment.

"Long ago, my people fought a war here against a being we called the Fallen," Gears said. "As part of that conflict, we established several armories on Earth. Most were ground to pieces by glaciers or now lie miles beneath the sea. But not all of them."

Gears stepped over the rubble that had fallen to the ground and through the doorway. Kevin scrambled after him. Gears retracted a panel on his silver chest plate and activated a powerful light, illuminating a rock-walled corridor that stretched before them.

"I studied ancient records to learn of this place," Gears said, his voice echoing off the walls as he led Kevin through the corridor. "My mission is to protect it. The Decepticons want the munitions within for their war, to use as weapons against us and against humans. They sent Reverb to stop me and secure the site for an invasion."

The corridor emptied into a dark chamber. Gears came to a sudden stop, and Kevin almost bumped into him. The giant robot increased his spotlight's intensity to maximum and shifted his upper body to move the light across the chamber. It was a cave about ninety feet across. Kevin saw piles of bizarre-looking cannons, missile launchers, and spiked weapons. He also saw strange-looking boxes and bulbous tubes and canisters, things whose purposes he couldn't even imagine. A long, cylindrical pillar of dark metal leaned against one wall. Everything was covered with dust.

"Alien weapons," Kevin said.

"Yes."

"When we left for Hawthorne, I thought your destination was a U.S. military ammo dump. Doesn't it seem odd that ancient aliens also used this area for storing weapons?"

"Yes," Gears said. "It is an odd coincidence. But in my experience, the universe is a place of many odd coincidences."

Kevin gestured to some of the more bizarre-looking artifacts and said, "So what do these things—"

"Silence," Gears said, raising one hand to motion Kevin to be still. Kevin listened. From down the length of the corridor behind them, he heard the *whump-whump-whump* of an approaching helicopter.

"It's probably the Army," Kevin said. "They must have seen the two tanks explode."

"I will present myself to them," Gears said. "Stay here." He limped back the way they'd come, dousing his light as he strode to the cave's exit.

Plunged into darkness, Kevin turned and ran after Gears. "Wait up!" he said. "You're not leaving me alone in the dark in a nineteen-thousand-year-old cave full of alien weapons!"

Gears glanced back at Kevin. "I have learned that arguing with you is futile, Kevin Bowman. At least stay behind me. Your species often shoots first and asks questions later."

They emerged from the corridor and stepped outside the cave. They saw a large black military helicopter sitting on the desert floor perhaps a hundred feet away, its rotors slowing to a halt. A squad of soldiers emerged from the helicopter, guns at the ready, followed by two yellow robots. Behind them came a third, chrome-armored Cybertronian, whose hands were manacled behind his back.

Kevin immediately recognized the prisoner as the one Gears had fought at the abandoned farm. *Reverb.* And he was looking straight at them with his red eyes.

"Gears!" Reverb yelled, bending and straining at his bonds as the other two new arrivals turned, their eyes fixed on the rocky hill where Gears and Kevin stood. The cuffs at Reverb's back shattered with a flare of red energy and he shouted, "Killer!"

Gears shifted his body protectively in front of Kevin and said, "Kevin! *Run!*"

Chapter Fourteen

"Killer!" Reverb shouted again as he threw the broken magnetic cuffs aside. Before Bumblebee and Ratchet could react, Reverb bolted away from the NEST helicopter and ran straight at Gears to renew their fight.

Neither Bumblebee nor Ratchet spotted the young boy who jumped away from the Cybertronian and tumbled behind a large rock. Gears ran back into the cave. Reverb followed him.

"Hold your fire!" Ratchet said to the nearby soldiers who had turned their rifles toward the rocky hill. Turning to Bumblebee, he said, "Let's go. Reverb may need our help against Gears."

"Whuuuh-uuuuuh-uuhh—" began Bumblebee, his vocal unit sputtering. He switched to their private channel. *"What if it's Gears who needs our help?"*

"Then why did he run away?" Ratchet asked skeptically. He signaled to a technician standing near the NEST helicopter. "Have we reestablished communications?"

"No, sir," the technician said, tapping his earpiece. "All channels are still out."

"Unfortunate," Ratchet said. "Prepare the liquid carbon-fiber tanks, and set up a defense net. We may need to immobilize whichever Cybertronian comes out of that cave."

"Yes, sir!"

Soldiers began scrambling and shouting. Bumblebee and Ratchet approached the cave's entrance warily.

A slight movement behind a nearby rock surprised Bumblebee and Ratchet. Adjusting their mechanical eyes, they saw a small human huddled there. The boy looked frightened, but he stood up away from the rock and yelled, "Are you Autobots or Decepticons?!"

"Awwwwwwww-toooooh..." began Bumblebee, then broke off in frustration.

"We're Autobots," Ratchet said. "Who are you?"

"Kevin Bowman."

"Are you all right? Did Gears harm you?"

"What? No! He saved my life *twice* tonight!" Pointing to the helicopter, Kevin continued, "Reverb was wearing big handcuffs. Why'd you let him loose on Gears? Don't you know Gears is an Autobot, too?"

"Reverb was our captive," Ratchet said. "He broke free. Kevin, can you tell us what's inside the cave?"

"It's filled with ancient weapons. Gears said his mission was to make sure Decepticons didn't get them. And you let Reverb go right in after him!"

Ratchet looked at Bumblebee and said, "I may have misjudged Reverb. But it is also possible that he is working *with* Gears, that their goal is to lure us into the cave."

"But I saw both of them fighting!" Kevin protested. "I'm telling you, they're *definitely* not friends! If you're Autobots, you have to help Gears!"

Ratchet looked at the mouth of the cave. "No

one else goes in there until I am certain of what we are up against."

When Gears raced into the cave, he knew he had only several seconds before Reverb caught up with him. He scanned a massive pulse cannon of ancient design, then scooped it up and held it against his chest. He plugged the cannon's dust-covered power leads into the circuits beneath his chest armor to try to power it up. He hoped the ancient Cybertronian technology was still functional.

The aged cannon managed to sputter to life, its indicators blinking green. Gears could feel its power, waiting to be used. Hearing heavy footsteps approach, he took cover beside a large container as he turned to aim the cannon at the corridor's entrance.

Reverb stepped into the chamber. His own sonic blaster was sticking out of his chest armor. His gaze swept over the weapons and equipment that were stacked in the chamber. Looking away from the container that concealed Gears's position, his eyes lingered for a moment on a long metal cylinder that rested against one wall. Ancient symbols, like hieroglyphs, were carved into it.

Although Gears had intended to fire at Reverb, he suddenly realized that a blast from the ancient cannon might bring the cave down on both of them. He opted for a more low-tech approach and jumped out from his hiding spot to bring his fist down hard across the back of Reverb's head and knocked him down.

As Reverb fell, he kicked out with one foot, driving it into the shin of Gears's damaged leg. Reverb rolled, but Gears fell on top of him, their chest-mounted cannons crashing into each other. Reverb threw his arms around Gears's head and hauled himself up so his cannon was braced against Gears's face. With triumph in his voice, Reverb said, "Good-bye, Gears."

"Go ahead," Gears said. "Do it. You will collapse this chamber on both of us, and Megatron will never get his hands on these weapons."

"Neither will Optimus Prime," Reverb sneered.

"Optimus Prime is not your concern," Gears said. "My mission was not to obtain the weapons. It was to stop you from doing so, and however possible." Gears brought one hand up fast, shoving Reverb's cannon aside as he jumped to his feet and clamped his hands on Reverb's wrists. And then it was Reverb who was staring down the barrel of his enemy's weapon.

Gears saw no reason to gloat or waste time. He activated his pulse cannon.

Nothing happened.

Gears saw his cannon's indicator lights were blinking red. He realized his chest-to-chest collision with Reverb had torn the power leads loose. As he clawed frantically at the disconnected circuitry, he activated his blue forearm mechanisms to shift his arm into a cannon. It was still unfolding when Reverb broke free from his grip, jumped back to get his footing, and opened fire.

The blast from Reverb's sonic cannon hit Gears with full force at almost-point-blank range, hurling him across the room. Gears slammed into the far wall so hard that the impact sent bits of rock and dust raining down from the cave's ceiling.

Gears collapsed, his huge limbs clattering as he fell to the floor.

Bumblebee, Ratchet, Kevin, and every soldier in the vicinity heard the thunderclap that erupted from the mouth of the cave. "Everybody down!" Ratchet yelled as he yanked Kevin off his feet and sprang away from the rocky hill alongside Bumblebee.

"Let go of me!" Kevin said as he tried to wriggle out of Ratchet's protective grasp. "Why aren't you going to help Gears?"

"If it is Gears who needs our help," Ratchet said, "I expect we will know soon enough."

The sound of approaching vehicles caused Ratchet and Bumblebee to look away from the rocky hill. They saw four U.S. Army military trucks approaching. The trucks stopped near the NEST helicopter, and armed soldiers spilled out from the trucks.

A commanding officer climbed out of one truck, faced the helicopter, and demanded,

"Who's in charge here?" But then the officer saw Ratchet and Bumblebee and said, "What the—are you two responsible for destroying our tanks?"

Ratchet released Kevin to go speak to the Army officer. Hitting the dirt, Kevin spotted a familiar face behind the wheel of a truck. Kevin ran to the truck and shouted, "Duane!"

Duane Bowman climbed out of the truck, looked at his brother with astonishment, and cried, "Kevin? What are you doing out here?" Glancing at his wristwatch, Duane added, "It's almost midnight. You said you were at Gilbert's!"

"It's a long story," Kevin said. Pointing to the cave entrance, he continued, "But a friend of mine is in that cave, and I'm afraid he's in big trouble. You have to help him!"

Chapter Fifteen
SECRET WEAPON

Inside the cave, Gears tried to rise. He managed to only jerk his arms slightly, and then they went slack again. Even without running diagnostics, he knew his systems were too damaged to mount any defense against Reverb.

Confident that he had vanquished Gears, Reverb walked slowly across the chamber, his glowing eyes scanning the ancient weapons. He picked up a pair of magnetizing cannons and secured them to both forearms, then lifted a missile launcher and hefted it onto his left shoulder. When his gaze fell upon an oval-shaped device, he said, "I haven't seen one of these in a long, long time." He secured the device to his metal waist, and a blanket of glowing light instantly appeared over most of his body. The device was a personal energy shield.

Examining his new weapons' indicators, Reverb said, "Excellent. Everything is in superb condition." Ignoring the immobilized Gears, he returned his attention to the dark metal cylinder. He studied its symbols, then cautiously extended one hand to touch it.

Gears managed to activate his vocal processor and stammered in a staticky voice, "Wh-wh-what is that?"

"It's a wuh-wuh-weapon," Reverb said mockingly. "It's what I was sent here for. It's the key to crushing you Autobots and your pathetic human allies." Reverb touched the cylinder tentatively.

"You're a-a-afraid of it," Gears said, hoping to buy time for Kevin and the others to get away.

Reverb chuckled. "If you knew what it did, Gears, you'd be afraid, too. Would you like a firsthand demonstration? I'd be happy to give you one." Reverb gripped the cylinder carefully, then hoisted it to rest horizontally upon his right shoulder. Mechanisms in his shoulder clicked as they shifted and locked onto the cylinder. Stepping back over to Gears, he grabbed Gears by the armor at his upper back and dragged him across the chamber.

"What are you doing?" Gears groaned.

Tapping the shoulder-mounted cylinder with his free hand, Reverb said, "Before I take this to Megatron, I need to test it. And what better targets than your friends?"

As Reverb hauled Gears from the chamber and into the corridor that led outside, Gears's mechanical eyes rolled in his head as he felt his Spark grow dim. He was painfully aware that he was entirely at Reverb's mercy. As he focused his concentration on his internal systems, all he could do was hope that Reverb was not in too great a hurry to destroy him.

Countless lives were at stake. Gears knew if he couldn't get himself in working order soon, all would be lost.

Outside the cave, Bumblebee, Ratchet, and the soldiers had fanned out, watching the mouth of the cave. Kevin was still trying to explain to his brother how he had traveled to Hawthorne when they heard heavy footsteps thudding from the cave.

"We'll talk later, Kevin," Duane said. "Take cover behind the truck!"

Kevin moved behind the Army vehicle and then looked back out to see Reverb lurch out of the darkness and stand in the mouth of the cave, dragging Gears behind him.

Bumblebee and Ratchet watched Reverb as he let his gaze travel over the figures who faced him. The Autobots noticed the strange, ancient weapons that were attached to Reverb and also the eerie glow of energy that surrounded his body. Neither Autobot was familiar with the cylinder-shaped object mounted on Reverb's shoulder. If they had any doubts about Reverb's affiliation with the Decepticons, those doubts vanished when Reverb let out an evil, grinding laugh.

Amplifying his own voice to be heard across the distance, Ratchet said, "Don't move, Reverb. Release Gears and remove your weapons or we will open fire."

Reverb laughed again. He let Gears fall to the ground inside the mouth of the cave and then removed the cylinder from his shoulder. He stood it on end in front of him, supporting it with one hand. "Destroy me?" Reverb shook his head. "I don't think so, Autobots. It's *you* who stand on the brink of destruction, and you deserve it...you and *all* of Optimus Prime's true believers. You disgrace the name *Cybertron* by making yourself servants of these pathetic, soft-shelled insects. But it is not too late. Repent of this foolishness, Autobots! Join the Decepticons and reclaim the destiny you have forgotten. We were born to rule the stars."

Bumblebee blasted ear-piercing static in indignation, but Ratchet raised one hand to silence his friend. "*We* were born to live in peace," Ratchet said, "as is the right of all sentient beings. We will defend that right as we have for millennia and sacrifice our lives to do so if we must."

Reverb responded with a nod. He didn't appear disappointed by Ratchet's refusal. If anything, he looked pleased. "So be it, Autobots," he said. He fired his sonic cannon at Ratchet and Bumblebee.

Ratchet and Bumblebee were far enough from Reverb that the blast knocked them both to their knees instead of flinging them across the plain. The Decepticon then began firing his other weapons, launching blasts of plasma and missiles that sent the Hawthorne soldiers and NEST commandos running for cover. The soldiers returned fire, but their bullets pinged off Reverb's energy shield, which only made Reverb laugh louder.

Ratchet and Bumblebee recovered and rushed Reverb, Ratchet sending a rapidly spinning blade from his arm like a ninja star while Bumblebee launched a sticky bomb. Both Autobots scored direct hits that merely glanced off Reverb's shield. Reverb returned fire, knocking Ratchet and Bumblebee off their feet again.

Gears remained sprawled and motionless on the ground behind Reverb. As his systems continued the agonizingly slow process of knitting themselves back together, he managed to flex his metal fingers, then moved his hand to the ancient plasma cannon still connected to his midsection. He closed his hand on the cannon shakily. Just his hand's short journey from the ground to the cannon had already nearly drained his power levels. He would have to wait a little longer to rejoin the fight.

Unaware of Gears's slight movement behind him, Reverb watched his opponents dive for cover and retreat across the desert. Sighting one group of soldiers, Reverb hoisted the ancient metal cylinder he'd taken from the cave, made some minute adjustments to controls embedded in the cylinder's surface, and then hurled the cylinder at the soldiers.

"Look out!" Ratchet shouted as the long object spiraled through the air. The cylinder appeared darker than dark, as if it were somehow pulling the available light into itself. Like a well-thrown spear, it embedded itself into the desert floor, but as it struck, it emitted a brilliant flash. Kevin was still hunkered down beside the truck when he saw the flash, and for a moment, he thought he saw glittering stars and swore he was seeing the night sky all over again in miniature. He even recognized the constellation he had been following, the Swan, but it was on the wrong side of the sky. And then, to his horror, the five soldiers who were closest to the cylinder began to cry out. Their bodies twitched, bending back involuntarily in the direction of the cylinder. And then the soldiers vanished.

One of the soldiers was Kevin's brother.

"Duane!" Kevin screamed.

The stars were suddenly gone. The cylinder now looked like nothing more than a pillar of metal stuck in the sand.

Ratchet and Bumblebee had seen the soldiers vanish, too. "Let's move," Ratchet said, "before Reverb can use that thing again."

The two Autobots rushed Reverb from either side, Bumblebee charging his plasma cannon and Ratchet extending his surgical saw. Reverb stepped away from Gears's motionless body, calmly dropped to one knee, and fired a missile at Ratchet. The missile caught Ratchet and spun him around, dropping him on his face in the dirt. Then Reverb turned the other way, just in time to see Bumblebee open fire. Plasma bounced crazily off Reverb's energy shield, leaving the Decepticon unharmed and Bumblebee dodging his own fire.

Reverb laughed in delight. He lunged for Bumblebee, snared his forearm, and hurled him over his head. Bumblebee crashed into the slope of the rocky hill and rolled through the dirt as Reverb's ancient pulse cannon tore craters in the desert behind him.

Reverb fired another missile at Ratchet, then

ran after Bumblebee. As Ratchet threw himself sideways, he saw the soldiers and NEST commandos taking cover behind their vehicles and the helicopter. He thought it was a wise move. Their weapons were useless against the powerful Decepticon.

Ratchet rolled to his feet and powered up his sharp-toothed saw as he ran after Reverb, who was closing ground on Bumblebee. He swung at the back of Reverb's neck, but the cutting tool never reached the Decepticon's armor. The saw hit the shield in a shower of sparks, and the impact flung Ratchet's arm backward.

Reverb turned and fired yet another missile at Ratchet, who ducked to the left, but Reverb predicted the move. Reverb kicked Ratchet hard, sending him crashing down. As Ratchet skidded across the ground, Reverb fired another round of missiles at Bumblebee.

With the battle moving away from the cave, Kevin raced to Gears's side. "You're hurt," Kevin said. "What can I do?"

"Run," Gears said weakly.

Kevin shook his head. "He killed my brother. He killed your friend. If someone doesn't stop him, he'll never stop killing."

"You cannot stop him," Gears said. "His shield is too powerful. We are beaten."

"No! There must be something we can do! Anything! Think, Gears! Think!"

"The power leads on my chest," Gears said. "Reattach them. I cannot lift my head to see them."

Three wires extended from the cannon lying across Gears's midsection. One was plugged into a socket inside the Autobot's exoskeleton. The others hung free. Kevin pushed the middle one into an empty socket. Gears shuddered.

Kevin said, "Did that hurt?"

"Yes. Keep going."

Kevin reattached the other power lead. Gears shuddered again. The indicator lights on the cannon blinked red and stayed that way.

"What's wrong?" Kevin said. "Why isn't it working?"

"The activation cycle is starting. But I doubt it will finish. The cannon has been damaged."

"So what do we do?"

"We wait."

Kevin, Gears, and the other Autobots heard a shrieking noise overhead. Ratchet felt a surge of hope when three attack helicopters streaked out across the night sky, lights flashing from their machine guns as they swooped down on Reverb. Explosive bullets flowered against the Decepticon's energy shield as he turned his head to face the helicopters, sizing up the new arrivals.

One helicopter fired a missile with a shriek of propellant. The projectile slashed a bright white line across the night sky, and when it smashed into Reverb, it appeared to change him into a ball of fire. But Reverb shrugged and the flames streamed away from him, rising into the air before they dissipated with a loud *whoosh*. Once again, Reverb's energy shield had held. Reverb turned to watch the helicopters and waited for them to make another pass.

While Reverb was preoccupied with the helicopters, Bumblebee looked at Ratchet and transmitted, *"Let's hit him together! Hard as we can!"*

"We just tried that. It didn't work."

Thinking fast, Bumblebee sent, *"Hit high and I'll hit him low. Let's see if we can pin him like we did back at the farm!"*

"You've come up with a lot of dumb plans,"

Ratchet replied, *"but this one just might be the dumbest."* Shaking his head, he said out loud, "Let's do it."

An attack helicopter fired two missiles at Reverb. The first missile streaked over his shoulder and blasted into the ground. The other smashed into his shield, with no more effect than anything else that anyone had thrown at him. Reverb fired his own shoulder-mounted missiles in response. Two missiles ripped through the helicopter's tail, sending it spinning out of control.

As the helicopter's pilot wrestled with his controls to make an emergency landing, Ratchet and Bumblebee made their move. They ran at Reverb, spinning, dodging, and leaping as he fired his cannons and missiles at them. Bumblebee reached Reverb first, diving to tackle his ankles. Sparks erupted as he contacted the energy shield. Bumblebee spasmed in pain, but he clung tight to the Decepticon's legs.

And then Ratchet, aiming for Reverb's head and chest, followed his friend by slamming into the shield. Ratchet's body shuddered violently as the shield's energy tore through his mechanical systems. The pain was much worse than when he'd hit the shield with his saw, but he maintained his footing beside Reverb and shoved hard.

Reverb fell down over Bumblebee. Ratchet fell atop Reverb's chest but was immediately flung backward by the shield, and then Reverb — lying on his back — kicked hard at Bumblebee's abdomen, sending him tumbling. Ratchet landed on his back in the sand a short distance from Reverb. Bumblebee came to a stop in the dirt about twenty feet away, sparks spitting from his shoulder and elbow joints.

Kevin, still kneeling beside his friend in the

rubble near the mouth of the cave, had been watching the confrontation in the desert between Reverb and Ratchet and Bumblebee, and he felt a sense of impending doom as he realized that the Autobots were losing. He looked at Gears, who slowly lifted his head slightly to peer at the indicator lights on the ancient plasma cannon. He urged the lights to turn green, but they continued to stubbornly blink red.

"The cannon is broken, Kevin," Gears said.

Reverb got to his feet and stood over Ratchet, who'd lifted himself to a sitting position. Ratchet tried to raise his arms and discovered he couldn't. He cursed his circuits.

"Such bravery," Reverb said, "and for what? A mudball world infested by insects." He put his foot on Ratchet's chest and pushed the Autobot down. Reverb extended his arm, and it changed into a long, sharp spike.

"Say good-bye, Ratchet," Reverb said as he drew his arm back. He was about to strike when he heard the *whump-whump-whump* of another helicopter approaching. But the massive military helicopter that moved across the sky wasn't from Hawthorne. And it wasn't carrying just human soldiers. As it neared Reverb and Ratchet's position, two large Autobots leaped out and landed on the ground.

Optimus Prime and Ironhide had arrived.

Chapter Sixteen
AUTOBOTS, ROLL OUT

"Gears!" Kevin cried beside his fallen friend. "Two more giant robots arrived! I think they're Autobots!"

Optimus Prime and Ironhide moved away from the large helicopter as it landed behind them. General Marcus and several NEST commandos jumped out of the helicopter and took up defensive positions alongside the remaining soldiers from the Hawthorne Army Depot. The two Autobots walked toward the rocky hill where a chrome-plated Decepticon outfitted with ancient weapons stood above the fallen Ratchet. To their left, Bumblebee was lying on the ground, sparks spitting from his arms.

Both Optimus and Ironhide saw the boy who was kneeling beside yet another Autobot in the shadowy cave entrance. Ironhide feared Optimus would want to negotiate with the Decepticon who loomed over Ratchet, but Optimus activated his weapons without breaking his stride, his cannons humming as they powered up. Ironhide saw that the boss meant business, and a fierce grin split his scarred metal face.

Reverb gave Ratchet a contemptuous kick, then swaggered forward to greet the new arrivals. "Well, if it isn't the king of the insects and his trigger-happy sidekick," Reverb sneered as he flexed the spike that still extended from his arm. "I shall enjoy presenting your disassembled parts to Megatron."

Ironhide had heard enough. "You're goin' down," he said, racing forward with his cannons blazing. Plumes of fire burst against Reverb's shield, and Reverb fired back a quartet of missiles. Ironhide ducked two missiles and leaped over a third, but the fourth struck him in the side, knocking him over.

Optimus Prime signaled to General Marcus and the commandos to stay back, and then his barrage cannon engaged with a roar. Optimus fired at Reverb, whose head and upper body seemed to vanish in a flash of white. But then the flash dissipated, and the Decepticon still stood where he was, unharmed.

"He's got an energy shield!" Ratchet yelled, earning another kick from Reverb. "Nothing can penetrate it!"

"We'll see about that!" Ironhide snarled, rushing Reverb from the side as Optimus scanned the Decepticon, noting the ancient weapons systems he wielded and seeking a weakness.

Reverb held his ground as Ironhide's missiles bounced off his shield. Ratchet tried to shout another warning as his friend advanced closer to Reverb, but his voice went unheard over the thunder of battle. Ironhide's fist connected with Reverb's shield, and he was instantly knocked backward, shouting in surprise at the violent shock.

Reverb advanced, preparing to fire his sonic cannon at Ironhide, but as he moved past Ratchet, the fallen warrior threw out one arm. Reverb tripped over Ratchet's arm as he fired. The sonic blast caught Ironhide in the legs instead of the chest, but the impact was still enough to send him tumbling across the desert. When he came to a stop, he groaned in pain.

Reverb turned to see Optimus Prime reaching for him with outstretched arms. Although many Decepticons would have run from the sight of the fierce Autobot leader, Reverb did not. Instead, he retracted his spike arm and grabbed hold of Optimus by both arms. Optimus adjusted his balance, leaning back on his legs, expecting Reverb to try to wrestle free of his grip. But instead, the Decepticon pulled Optimus toward him, into the deadly shield.

Optimus's body shook as red bolts of energy danced across his armor, sending sparks out of the joints of his limbs. Reverb held him in his awful embrace for a full ten seconds, then let go. Ratchet watched in horror as the mighty Optimus Prime fell to his knees, then crumpled to the ground.

Kevin gasped as he watched the huge Autobot fall, and then Reverb began pounding at the Autobot's armor. The soldiers began firing at Reverb, but their bullets pinged off his shield and ricocheted toward the rocks, kicking up dirt and blasting stones near Kevin.

"Hold your fire!" General Marcus shouted. "You'll hit the boy!"

A desperate possibility occurred to Kevin. Looking at Gears, he said, "Do you have enough power to generate another hologram?"

"Leave this place, Kevin," Gears muttered. "Now . . . you must leave now."

"I said, *can you generate a hologram*?"

"Maybe . . . maybe for a few seconds."

Kevin said, "Remember your friend Tailgate?"

Gears heard Reverb's fists still hammering away at Optimus Prime. Gears said, "Yes. I remember. . . ."

"Make a hologram of him! Project it over me, make it follow my movements, and give me his voice!"

"This will not work, Kevin," Gears said sadly. "You will be killed."

"Do you think Reverb will let me live anyway? After what I've seen? Do you think he'll let *any* of us live?"

Gears sighed. He thought of Tailgate, of his bright orange armor and his graceful movements, and how full of life he had been. And as he remembered Tailgate, he studied Kevin's face and said, "You are very brave."

And then Gears brought Tailgate's hologram to life, shifting the three-dimensional image of a large Cybertronian over Kevin's body. Kevin stepped away from Gears and called out, "Reverb!"

Rising away from Optimus Prime, Reverb

turned in response to the voice. When he saw the Autobot standing a short distance from the cave's entrance, his mouth fell open with astonishment. Reverb muttered in disbelief, "Tailgate?"

"It's been a long time, Reverb."

"It...it can't be," Reverb said. "Your Spark was extinguished! I saw it go out!"

Kevin placed his hands on his hips, and the hologram of Tailgate did the same as Gears matched his movements. "There are more powerful things in this cave than you can imagine," he said.

"Not *that* powerful," Reverb said, but his voice quavered uncertainly. "The dead stay dead!"

"Come see for yourself....If you're brave enough."

Reverb watched Tailgate retreat into the cave. Still not quite believing what he'd just seen,

Reverb looked around. He saw Optimus Prime trying to rise and failing. The other Autobots were scattered on the ground.

Reverb could not imagine that any of them would recover while he went after Tailgate in the cave. After all, he had brought down Optimus Prime. He was invincible.

The hologram of Tailgate flickered and faded a moment after Kevin entered the cave. As he proceeded deeper into the darkness, he heard Reverb's heavy feet following him.

He hurried down the pitch-black corridor, heading for the weapon-filled chamber. Perhaps there was some weapon there he could activate, some way he could bring the cave crashing down on top of Reverb, entombing him under stone.

Although Kevin knew it would mean his own death, Reverb—the Decepticon who had taken Duane's life—would be defeated. It was a sacrifice Kevin was willing to make.

Keeping his right arm out in front of him, he dragged his left hand along the corridor's wall to help guide him to the inner chamber. He moved fast to get ahead of the enemy.

In the mouth of the cave, Reverb's foot came down beside Gears's head. Reverb stood there as he scanned for any sign of Tailgate. He took another step forward, his feet now planted on either side of Gears's head. He did not bother to look down because he considered Gears no more of a threat than the other fallen Autobots.

Gears shifted his gaze to look up at Reverb.

And then he saw the indicator lights on the ancient cannon on his chest finally flashing intermittent green. The weapon's startup sequence was nearly complete.

Come on, Gears thought. *Come on, come on, come on, come on!* He shifted his hands to the cannon to tilt it up.

Reverb lifted his foot to step over Gears.

The indicator lights turned solid green.

Gears fired.

The damaged cannon didn't roar—it was more like a cough, spitting bright blue energy from its muzzle. But Gears was in a perfect position, directly below Reverb. The shield covered most of his body, but it didn't extend *underneath* him. The blast caught the Decepticon in the undercarriage, launching him up to the roof of the cave. Reverb bounced off the ceiling and fell, crashing face-first onto the corridor floor. A blue flash surrounded Reverb, then vanished.

Stunned, Reverb pushed himself up from the ground. He realized his energy shield was gone, the ancient shield generator ruined. Turning back to Gears, he roared in fury as he bent down and tore the still-smoking ancient cannon off Gears's midsection. He picked up Gears and flung his body away into the desert in a rage, then ran after him. When Gears tumbled to a stop, Reverb jumped on top of him. Once again, Reverb changed one arm into a long spike. He was about to plunge the spike into Gears's metal head when a deep voice said, "Stop."

Reverb looked away from Gears to see Optimus Prime walking slowly toward him. The Decepticon opened fire with his cannons, dropping Optimus to his knees. He was about to spring when Ironhide managed to fire a missile that streaked out of the night and caught Reverb in the shoulder, sending him spinning away from Gears.

Seeing Reverb go tumbling, Ironhide shouted, "Boss! His shield's down!"

Optimus Prime got back up. Reverb jumped to his feet, but he wasn't fast enough. Optimus seized him and threw him down to the ground before he wrenched the ancient cannons off his forearms.

"Enough," Optimus said.

Reverb head-butted the Autobot in the chest, and Optimus responded by punching him in the face. Reverb fired a missile from his undamaged launcher. It ripped a crater in the ground behind Optimus's head, sending dirt raining down over the battlefield.

Optimus planted his foot on Reverb's chest and tore the ancient missile launcher out of the

Decepticon's hands, hurling it aside. Reverb threw his own body up from the ground, knocking Optimus backward and into the crater made by the missile strike. The Decepticon powered up his sonic cannon before he jumped into the crater after Optimus, failing to notice that Optimus had turned his own right arm into a battle blade.

Reverb screamed as the battle blade was driven through his falling body. The Decepticon's sonic cannon emitted a squeal of feedback and fell silent.

Kevin rushed out of the cave and saw the Autobot and Decepticon in the crater. He fell to his knees beside Gears and said, "Are you all right?"

Gears managed a mechanical smile and replied, "I am repairable."

Optimus Prime climbed out of the crater,

dragging Reverb by the leg. He looked down at the Decepticon's battered torso and saw a blinking mechanism that he recognized as a wide-range communications jammer. Optimus reached into Reverb's exoskeleton and yanked it out.

"That should clear the air," Optimus said.

He ran a quick test with his communications systems and confirmed that he was picking up thousands of transmissions again.

"Go ahead," Reverb said, his voice weak but still full of hate. "You have defeated me. Now destroy me. Take my Spark."

"That is not our way," Optimus Prime said. "But you are now a prisoner." He activated his communicator and ordered the NEST commandos to bring the carbon-fiber tanks as quickly as possible. Reverb would have to be immobilized until he could be interrogated.

Optimus looked away from the crater and saw Ironhide walking slowly across the desert, arms hanging limply by his sides. "Only a scratch, boss," the battered Autobot said.

"Of course," Optimus said. "Watch over him, Ironhide." Leaving the crater, he walked slowly over to where Ratchet and Bumblebee were sprawled on the ground. Looking at Ratchet, he said, "Can you get up?"

"Just give me a minute," Ratchet said. "How are you doing, Bumblebee?"

Using a song to communicate, Bumblebee replied, "*I do pretty well, till after sundown.*"

"You fought well," Optimus said proudly. While Ratchet helped Bumblebee up, Optimus walked to the other Autobot, the one who had been lying motionless when he'd arrived. Kevin looked up as Optimus lowered himself to one knee and said, "I am Optimus Prime."

"I'm Kevin Bowman," the boy said, extending his hand. Optimus reached down and touched Kevin's hand gently with one enormous metal finger. Kevin brushed his other hand across Gears's shoulder and added, "And this is Gears."

Optimus said, "It is an honor to meet such brave soldiers."

Looking toward Ironhide at the crater, Kevin said, "What are you going to do with Reverb?"

"We must find out what he knows."

Choking back tears, Kevin said, "He killed my brother, Duane, and also four other men. He did it with that weapon." Kevin pointed to the strange metal cylinder that was still sticking out of the ground.

"Excuse me," Optimus said as he rose away from Kevin and Gears. He went to the cylinder and examined it carefully without touching it.

Looking back to Kevin, he said, "This is not a weapon."

"What is it, then?" Kevin said. "I'm telling you, that thing made five men disappear. I saw it happen. They were vaporized."

"I am not so certain of that," Optimus said. "I know of devices that match the appearance of this relic. This device may have opened a gateway through space and dragged your brother and the other men through it."

Looking at the cylinder, Kevin said dubiously, "A gateway? A gateway to *where*?"

Optimus shook his head. "I do not know. But very far from here, I suspect."

"Then...Duane could still be alive?"

Optimus looked up at the stars, then returned his gaze to Kevin. "I will not lie to you, Kevin Bowman. I can only imagine the chances are low that your brother and the others were transported to a habitable place with a breathable atmosphere. And even if they are still alive, the chances of bringing them home are... unlikely. I am sorry."

"I understand," Kevin said. "But you said *unlikely*. You didn't say *impossible*."

"No," Optimus Prime said. "It is not impossible."

"Then there's hope?"

Optimus nodded. "Yes, Kevin. There is always hope."

Chapter Seventeen

"No," General Marcus said. "Absolutely not. It's out of the question. We can't take the boy with us."

After the NEST commandos secured the ancient munitions stronghold and encased the immobilized Reverb in layers of carbon fiber, it was well after midnight. The NEST helicopters prepared to leave Hawthorne and return to Edwards Air Force Base. Bumblebee, Ratchet, and Ironhide were resting quietly beside the helicopters while techs worked on repairing their systems. Gears was laid out on a flatbed truck that had been brought in from Hawthorne. General Marcus stood beside the truck, facing Optimus Prime and Kevin.

"I do not wish to argue with you, General Marcus," Optimus Prime said, "but Kevin Bowman has informed us that his parents are dead and that his brother is his only surviving relative." Optimus gestured to a military truck. "We have secured the artifact that may have transported Kevin's brother and four other men to another world. For all we know, Kevin may somehow be a key to recovering his brother, and—"

"*If* those men can be recovered," General Marcus interjected.

"They're alive," Kevin said. "I know they are!"

Optimus gestured at Gears and continued, "General, Gears told us how Kevin Bowman helped him travel to Hawthorne. It was Kevin's idea to use a hologram to divert Reverb. He is intelligent as well as resourceful. He is a good ally."

"He's just a kid!" General Marcus protested.

"I have met other young humans like him. The young can often see what we do not. And where would you send him, General Marcus? Back to an empty home? Or would you rather he—"

"Blazing bombs!" General Marcus cursed. "All right, fine. The boy comes with us. I'll personally notify local authorities in case any of his friends or neighbors report him missing. I'll even set him up with a tutor so he doesn't fall behind in school. But he's *your* responsibility, Optimus! And if he goes on any missions with you, those missions are classified!"

From the flatbed, Gears said, "When I am repaired, I will assume responsibility for Kevin Bowman."

Despite his bluster, General Marcus grinned as he looked at Kevin and said, "Listen to that, son. They're already fighting over who gets to keep you." He turned to an aide. "All right, let's wrap this up and go home!"

Optimus faced Kevin and said, "You will be all right, Kevin. And we will do everything we can to find your brother."

"Thanks," Kevin said. He lifted himself up onto the flatbed so he was close to Gears's head and said, "If you're still trying to get rid of me, you're doing a lousy job."

Gears looked up at the stars overhead. "I would like to know more about your constellations," he said. "Perhaps you will teach me?"

"I can do that."

In a mansion outside Sparks, Nevada, an encrypted cell phone rang with a dull chime. The cell phone's owner was seated behind his desk when he heard the chime. He lifted the phone, held it to the side of his head, and said, "This is Stealth Leader. Go ahead."

"I've returned to base," Simon Clay replied. "But we have ground reports of a clash at the Hawthorne Army Depot. Our asset failed and was captured. The mission was a total loss."

"No," said Stealth Leader into the phone. "It was a success. We have learned much about the critical technology for Project Nightbridge. The primary objective was achieved. All other objectives were secondary."

"I don't understand," Clay said.

"It's not your job to understand," Stealth Leader said testily. "All you need to know is this: The fight against the Autobots has just begun."

Clay started to say something else, but Stealth Leader was done talking.

Douglas Porter broke the connection and placed the phone on his desk. The teenager with perfect hair put his hands behind his head, leaned back in his chair, and contemplated his next move.